OVER A BARREL

A Table for Two Novella

LAYLA REYNE

Over a Barrel

Copyright © 2023 by Layla Reyne

E-Book ISBN: 979-8-9869229-2-8

Print ISBN: 979-8-9869229-9-7

Cover Design: Cate Ashwood Designs; Cover Photo: Wander Aguiar; Editing: Adam Mongaya; Proofreading: Lori Parks

Content Warnings: Explicit language; explicit sex including consensual D/s dynamic, voyeurism, and exhibitionism; on-page and off-page instances / discussion of homophobia, misogyny, and antisemitism; on-page discussion of past child abuse and heart condition of secondary characters.

At your mercy this holiday season…

Ingredients:
One feisty redheaded attorney guarding her heart and her friends' business interests.
One bossy seasoned negotiator who always gets what she wants.
A distillery at the center of a contested year-end deal that pits two fierce women against each other.

Directions:
Mash ingredients in New Orleans with family and holiday cheer to bring down their walls.
Add mutual professional challenges and a steamy desire to burn hot together in public.
Be careful to avoid last-minute changes that will upset the deal and risk combustion.

Unless the blend is strong enough to withstand the heat—a full proof love perfect for aging.

Take a shot of this sexy age-gap F/F romance novella and raise your glass for festive sapphic cheer.

For Susan, Anna, and Laura,
who bravely paved their own way in the legal field and
helped me find my way too

Chapter One

Al was a sucker for a redhead. Always had been, always would be, didn't matter when or where.

Case in point: she was through airport security, halfway down the concourse on her way to the boarding gate, when a flash of auburn drew her gaze to the striking white woman at the bar. Wild curls of dark red cascaded down her back, designer jeans hugged her ass and thighs, and an emerald green sweater hung precariously askew on her shoulders.

Al could continue the rest of the way to her gate and video chat with her grandkids, check in with the family winery, or answer any of the hundred or so emails that awaited her return to work tomorrow. *Or*, if Red at the bar was game, Al could flirt her way into a bathroom stall and in between those denim-clad thighs before her flight.

The woman shifted on her chair, and her sweater slipped fully off one shoulder. Freckles. Fucking kryptonite. Al's fate was sealed.

Al hitched her purse firmly onto her shoulder and skirted through the gap in the bar's faux patio enclosure. Weaving through the pub tables, she sidled up to Red. "This seat taken?"

The other woman glanced up from her laptop, and if the freckles hadn't been a sharp enough hook, the warm brown eyes would've done the trick. Surprised, she glanced around, her gaze lingering a second longer on the empty table beside them before landing back on Al. "Uh, sure . . ."

Sounded more like a question, which Al answered by climbing onto the other chair. Pub tables were tricky at five foot two, trickier in a maxi skirt and travel flats, but with multiple restaurants in the family, Al had learned to manage. She hooked her purse on the chair back, then righted herself in time to catch Red's gaze roaming over her with interest. A positive sign.

"What's good here?" Al asked.

"It's an airport bar." She closed her laptop and leaned back in her chair. "Nothing's good here."

Al smirked and eyed the empty cocktail glass on the table. "Not even the drinks?"

She wobbled her hand. "Shit for vermouth, but at least when I order a Manhattan, I don't have to tell the bartender it's supposed to be rye." The lady knew her cocktails; Al liked that. "Your first time through here?"

"SFO?" Al shook her head. "No, but it is my first time in this bar. You?"

"Good Lord, no." She chuckled, and the husky tone of it sent a bolt of lust straight to Al's clit. "Pretty sure the staff knows me by name."

"Frequent flyer?"

She nodded. "Especially this time of year. I'm from Half Moon Bay, so back and forth for the holidays. You?"

"New York," Al answered, "if the accent didn't give it away."

One corner of Red's mouth curled up, her half smile reserved and devastatingly attractive. "It did, but I wasn't going to say."

"Ah, manners, and I'm forgetting mine." She extended a hand across the table. "I'm Al."

"CC." Returning the handshake, she didn't jerk away when Al swiped a thumb across the underside of her wrist. Another positive sign. Her sly smirk was an even better one. "Are you always this forward?"

"Did you miss the New York part?" Which included the unfailing ability to flag down cabs and servers. She drew back and hailed one of the latter. She passed on the seasonal eggnog martini and ordered another Manhattan for CC and one for herself. "Like you said," Al replied to her raised brow. "Forward."

"Fair," CC said with another of those sexy laughs. "Though my sister's the same way, and she's one hundred percent California girl."

"Older or younger?"

Brown eyes rolled, and a heavy sigh followed. "Younger."

"Oh," Al drawled, leaning forward on her forearms. CC's eyes strayed to her cleavage and lingered long enough for Al to consider it the final sign she needed to continue Mission Flirt-Her-Way-Between-Those-Thighs. "There's a story there."

CC's half smile grew, full of affection with a dash of exasperation. "She's my best friend and housemate. I love her dearly, but she's a *lot*. If it weren't for the pastries, I might have disowned her by now."

Al waited for the server to drop off their drinks before asking, "Pastries?"

"She's a pastry chef. The one thing that's ever stuck for her."

"You hit the jackpot." She lifted her glass, and CC clinked the rim against hers.

"You have no idea." She sipped at her drink, then lowered the glass, a French-manicured nail circling the rim as her mind drifted, along with her words. "I'm not sure I would have survived 1L without her." Then, as if catching herself, she redirected her attention to Al. "I'm sorry, I meant—"

"First year of law school," Al said, the lingo coming naturally to her as well. "Columbia Law, class of 1992."

"Stanford Law, 2004."

"Won't hold that against you," Al said with a wink. Drink in hand, she rested back in her chair and crossed her legs under the table. Close enough CC could make the next move. "But let's not talk about work. I don't want to remember I have to go back to it tomorrow."

"Were you out here for Thanksgiving?"

Al nodded. "My son's family is in San Francisco, and my ex-husband owns a winery in Sonoma. His new husband is a chef, so he got the big cooking holiday."

CC quirked a brow. "And all that was drama-free?"

"Well, I don't know." Al tapped the rim of her own glass with her fingertip. "Do you consider a four-year-old and two-year-old painting the walls with gravy drama?"

CC nearly spit out her drink. Hand clamped over her mouth, she managed to swallow, then gasped through her fingers with laughter. "For real?"

"For real." Al set aside her glass and splayed her hands, remembering how her grandkids had done the same, so proud of their work. "Award-winning gravy, all over the tasting room."

CC lowered her hand, and her face, relaxed with laughter, was breathtaking. So was her leg brushing against Al's beneath the table and staying there. "At least you don't own the place."

"Oh, but I do. Fifty percent of it."

"Just so you know"—CC leaned forward and lowered her voice, whispering conspiratorially—"you might not get your investment back. I do food and beverage law. The chance of winery success is slim."

"I've been warned, and I've seen it as a real estate attorney too." She matched CC's posture, the shift an excuse to drag her leg along CC's, the rough denim of her jeans firing all of Al's senses—and CC's too, judging by the beautiful blush that appeared at the collar of her sweater, creeping north. "But I owed him a midlife crisis, and at least this way one of us is close to the grandkids."

"Also fair," CC conceded with a sexy smile. "And you've got a vineyard and free wine whenever you want."

Her easy, enticing grin reeled Al the rest of the way in.

She finished her drink, leaned closer, and uncrossed her legs so she could use a knee to part CC's beneath the table. She pressed her knee against CC's inner thigh, intentions clear. "You know what else I might want?"

CC's gaze flared with heat and didn't waver as she used her manicured nails to fish the dark cherry out of her glass and pop it in her mouth. She scooted forward in her chair, and Al's knee slid higher. "What's that?"

An invitation to a bathroom stall was on the tip of Al's tongue when her phone blared from her purse behind her. Her eyes slipped closed on a frustrated growl. "For my phone not to ring when I'm trying to pick up a beautiful woman at the bar."

CC chuckled, the husky tone doing nothing for Al's thwarted libido. "They make a vibrate and silent function for that."

She opened her eyes again, meeting the dancing brown ones across from her. "Which I failed to use, and that ringtone is for the gravy monsters who are too cute at this age to ignore."

"Go." CC straightened, taking the heated contact and promise of more away. "I need to make a quick call before my flight too."

Al climbed off the pub chair and extended a hand to the redhead that would get away. "It was a pleasure meeting you, CC."

"Likewise." This time it was CC who slowly dragged a thumb over the inside of Al's wrist, and another bolt of lust arrowed right between Al's thighs. "And thanks for the compliment."

Al lifted the beauty's hand and kissed the back of it. "Only wish I'd had the chance to give you more."

Chapter Two

Al hated to be *that* person. The one the gate agent had to call over the loudspeaker and corral onto the plane. But once she profusely apologized and showed the agent, then the flight attendants the screenshots of Molly and Michael tangled in popcorn strings and tinsel, squaring off with dreidels for swords, in front of the Christmas tree decked out in blue and white lights, all was forgiven.

Besides, the plane door was still open, a member of the ground crew checking cockpit dials while the pilots ate their dinner. She wasn't the cause of the delay, but the other first-class passengers didn't seem to care about that reality. They all shot her nasty glares, which she returned with a flirty wave, making them frown harder.

Except for the person in the last row of first class who muffled a laugh. The attractive husky sound drew Al's attention, then her smile, as she eyed the redhead who apparently hadn't gotten away. And who was in the window seat next to the only vacant seat left in first class—Al's.

She tucked her purse in the overhead bin and slid into her cushy seat next to CC's. "You think they'd let me back off the plane to buy a lottery ticket?"

CC grinned. "That might be pushing it."

"When we land in New Orleans, then. Because this"—she gestured between them—"is some good luck."

CC's throaty laugh continued to entice her, but Al had to hold that thought; the flight attendant was already cruising through the cabin, taking meal and drink orders for when they were in the air, then collecting glasses and trash once the cockpit and airplane doors were finally closed.

"I thought you were headed to New York," CC said as the plane pushed back from the gate.

"I'm from New York. My firm is there too, but I've been seconded with a client in New Orleans for almost a year now."

"Long secondment."

Longer than Al had anticipated, but her sabbatical from the city was doing her and her client good. "They're in growth mode," she said, referring to her client. "And New Orleans is not a bad place to be seconded."

"You'll get no argument from me. I went to Tulane for my LLM and never left."

They continued to chat through takeoff and over drinks and dinner, CC's lovely blush reappearing on her cheeks and across her collarbones whenever Al paid her a compliment. Al wanted to see how much rosier she could make all that peaches and cream skin. And judging by CC's gaze that kept straying to Al's cleavage and the lingering brush of their shoulders and hands time and again, CC remained just as interested as she had been at the bar, if not more so. Mission Flirt-Her-Way-Between-Those-Thighs was still a go, but Al would need to make some adjustments given the vanishing space in airplane bathrooms.

The next time the attendant passed their row, making his last postdinner walk-through before they dimmed the lights for the rest of the flight, Al asked for a blanket.

CC's "You don't look cold," whispered hotly in her ear, was the last green light Al needed. She shifted so CC's lips brushed the shell of her ear, and goose bumps raced across Al's skin, exactly as she'd intended. CC chuckled. "That's manufacturing evidence."

Al turned her head, bringing them nose to nose, their breaths mingling in the narrow space between them. "I thought you said you did food and beverage law."

"And if you've been practicing in New Orleans for a year, you've had to have taken the bar, so you should know better."

Al scrunched her nose. "Pesky evidence rules."

CC's grin was red-hot, but before Al could lean the rest of the way over the seat divider and taste it, someone behind them cleared his throat. "Ma'am," the attendant said. "I have that blanket for you."

Rotating in her seat, she smiled at the attendant and took the blanket, setting it in her lap. "Thank you."

"Do you need anything else?"

"We're all set. Enjoy that book you were reading."

"Oh, I will!" He grinned and scurried back to the front.

The lights dimmed a moment later and the seat-back televisions flickered to life with entertainment options. Al waited until the attendant clicked in his seat belt before checking the row opposite her and CC. The older man in the aisle seat was already dozing off, and the younger person by the window had their earbuds in and their attention fixated on their e-reader. Good. She rotated back to find CC resting comfortably in her seat, albeit closer to her than the window, the boatneck of her sweater having fallen off her shoulder.

Al ached to kiss it. She handed her the blanket instead.

"This you giving me more?" CC asked.

Al trailed a fingertip over her exposed shoulder, watching with delight as heat rushed to meet her touch. "No, Red, me giving you more would have been taking you into a bathroom stall at SFO and finger fucking you until you came so I could see more of this beautiful blush."

CC's eyes flared with heat, and she squirmed in her seat, spreading her legs to no doubt ease the same pressure building between Al's.

"You would have liked that?" Al said.

CC bit her bottom lip, and fuck if Al didn't want to kiss that too. CC let it go with a swipe of her tongue. Someone liked to tease. "It's a shame airplane bathrooms are so small these days."

"Amen to that." Al leaned over the divider and dropped her voice low. "But we don't need a bathroom if you want to play."

CC inhaled sharply, then made a lap with her gaze around the first-class cabin. When her warm brown eyes landed back on Al, they were blistering.

"You like that too?" Al asked. CC nodded, and Al made a mental note to buy two lottery tickets when she got off the plane. Wasn't every day she found someone who got the same thrill she did from other eyes in the room, whether they were watching or not. She crossed her legs in CC's direction and propped a forearm on the seat divider, leaning over more and plumping her breasts. CC's gaze shot right to her cleavage, as Al expected it would. "Eyes up here, Red."

CC's muffled groan of frustration was adorable. And hot as hell. "Your tits are amazing."

"I know they are. Paid good money for them. You're a breast woman?"

"Among other things."

"Would you like to suck on them?"

Her eyes darted up from where they'd strayed again. "We can't—"

"No, we can't," Al admitted regretfully. She trailed a finger down her sternum, nudging the V-neck of her sweater lower, more of her breasts and a hint of her black satin bra cups showing. "But you can imagine them spilling over the black leather corset I have at home while you spread that blanket over your lap."

CC's blush grew redder, her breaths shorter, even as she hesitated, her gaze making another lap around the cabin.

"Trust me," Al coaxed. "I've got you, Red."

She spread the blanket over her lap and left a hand under the cover.

"That's good, CC."

CC's shy smile, the dip of her chin, was utterly charming. She liked praise too—*three* lottery tickets.

Al shifted so more of her back was to the aisle, then stretched out an arm and laid her hand over CC's other one on her thigh. Keeping the blanket in place for what she had planned. "Now undo your fly and slide a hand inside your jeans, over your underwear."

CC's hand moved under the blanket, unfastening, then unzipping her fly. She spread her legs farther apart, and Al knew the exact moment when CC dipped her hand lower. Head back, she sighed in relief, and her torso and shoulders sank into the seat. She was letting go, putting her trust in Al.

"You're doing so good. Feels good too, doesn't it?" CC nodded as Al traced soft patterns on the back of her hand still above the blanket. "Tell me how you feel."

"So hot. Even through the silk."

"They're silk, hmm?" With her other hand, Al wrapped a finger around the shiny green bra strap threatening to fall off CC's shoulder, like the sweater of the same color. "Matching with this?"

CC bit her bottom lip and nodded.

"They designer too, like your jeans and sweater?"

"I like nice things."

"I think you like naughty things. Let me guess. Thong?"

Auburn lashes fluttered open, and the hooded eyes

that swung in Al's direction should've been illegal in all fifty states.

"Oh, Red, if I'd gotten you in that bathroom stall, I would've fisted that scrap of silk, yanked it aside, and been knuckle-deep in you before you could even gasp."

CC did gasp then, and her hand made a sudden dip beneath the blanket. Didn't take a genius to know CC had gone off plan.

Al clasped her other hand on top of the blanket. "Did I tell you to put your fingers inside yet?"

"Please."

"Well, at least you've got them good and wet now. Pull them out and rub your clit over the silk." She made a swirling motion on the back of CC's hand, simulating what she wanted CC to do. "Dirty up those designer panties for me."

The sound that escaped CC's lips was half hiss, half moan.

Al continued weaving the fantasy. "Imagine your fingers are my tongue. That we're in that bathroom stall, that I went to my knees for you. Cinched that thong tight so I could use my tongue to play with it over your clit."

"Fuck."

"Swollen?"

She nodded, but she kept moving her hand beneath the blanket as directed. Her head lolled toward Al, her shorter breaths puffing over Al's knuckle where her finger was still woven in the green silk strap. She pulled tighter and leaned closer. "My clit's swollen too, Red. Has been since you laughed at the bar. But now, fuck, I'm drenched too, just thinking about how wet you must be between those amazing thighs, what it would feel like to have my fingers buried inside that hot heat. I'd get them soaked, then glide them up either side of your clit, teasing you right to the edge, before plunging them back inside you for another hit."

Her breath stuttered. "Can I?"

"Yeah, baby, dip your fingers inside your underwear. Tell me how wet you are."

"Fuck, I'm soaked." Her hips rocked, teasing and torturing herself, like Al wanted to do to CC and herself.

She shifted her hand on top of the blanket, moving it higher, palming the inside of CC's thigh. "I'd have hitched this leg up and finger fucked you with one hand." CC keened, tilting closer, her tongue licking Al's knuckle. She extended the finger, and CC didn't hesitate to suck it between her lush lips. Al nearly lost her mind, trembling and shifting as her own clit throbbed.

But she could wait; she was a Domme, and this was what she did. Doled out the pleasure for her sub before taking her own. She took back her finger after a few glorious seconds. "Stuff yourself full, baby. Imagine it's my wet fingers jammed inside you. Imagine my other hand wrapped around all your gorgeous hair, holding your naughty mouth to my tit"—she bent up a knuckle for CC to latch onto with her mouth—"so you could suck through the scream when I make you *come*."

CC's lips closed tight around her knuckle, teeth digging in just shy of painful, as the rest of her body tensed, jerking as much as Al's hand on her thigh allowed as her climax crashed through her.

She came back down after a minute, relaxing into the seat. Al helped situate her and righted her bra strap and sweater. "I don't know," Al mused. "Maybe this was better than the bathroom stall."

CC's postorgasm smile was her undoing. Patience shot, Al uncrossed her legs and shifted to the end of her seat. Before she could stand, though, CC clasped her wrist, confusion wrinkling her brow. "Where are you going?"

"To get you some water."

Her worry lines smoothed, and she relaxed back in the seat, releasing her hold. "Thank you."

"No, Red, thank you." Al brushed a stray auburn strand off her beautiful seatmate's sweaty forehead. "After I get your water, I'm gonna go to the bathroom, hike up my skirt, and shove three fingers into my drenched cunt, and I'm gonna fuck myself while imagining it's you on your knees eating me out."

Dazed eyes fluttered open. "I'm a cunt woman too."

Al winked. "Good to know."

Chapter Three

CC waited at one of the tasting room's pub tables, scrolling through texts while sipping her favorite dark rye. One of the distillers had poured a glass for her before returning to the working distillery that occupied most of the building. The once-crumbling structure, an 1800s Creole-style church, had been restored to its former glory, updated with modern utilities and outfitted with everything needed to run a top-shelf distillery and tasting room. It was one of CC's favorite places in New Orleans. Hands down her favorite local whiskey. As her thumb hovered over her text thread with Al from that morning, she wondered if the other woman had ever been here. She appreciated a good drink. She would appreciate an operation like Tchin Tchin and the whiskeys they made.

Maybe see how Friday goes first, her sister, Colby, gently chided in her head. Which made no sense, as Col was the more impulsive of the two of them. But Colby was also fiercely protective and the person who had rescued CC after her last failed relationship.

Colby was right, she should wait until Friday.

But Al's texts . . .

She opened the messages from that morning, recalling her excitement and relief at finally hearing from Al. They'd exchanged numbers at the airport before heading their separate ways, but there had been no texts or calls since then. CC had started to text Al a half dozen times herself, usually each night after she got herself off to the memory of their encounter on the plane or each morning when she woke, panties soaked after another night dreaming of Al's tits or the fantasy Al had put in her head of CC on her knees eating Al out.

She shifted on her pub stool. Now was not the time for any of those fantasies. But come Friday . . .

You know Dram in the Bywater? Al's text read.

CC had laughed out loud and in text.

What's so funny, Red?

Al hadn't been the first person to call her Red, but unlike with others, *Red* in Al's accent, the usually abrasive tone moderated by attentiveness, sophistication, and confidence—sexual and otherwise—sent a wave of heat rippling through CC. She had slipped a hand between her legs that morning, through the moisture already there, and spread it around her clit as she'd continued to text with her other hand. **Yeah, I know it. My sister is the pastry chef there.**

Wait? Your sister is Colby?

The very same.

The facepalm emoji had appeared, followed by the laughing one. **Should've put it together. The hair, the eyes, the rocking bodies.** A pause, then Al had added, **You WERE spoiled. Your sister's talent with pastry dough is sinful.**

Wait until the sufganiyot appear.

CC didn't replay the voice memo of Al groaning, "Fuck me." Earlier, it had sent CC's fingers plunging into her cunt. Not an option now as she waited for her clients.

If my daughter-in-law had met her before Tyler, Al's texts had resumed, **I probably wouldn't have my grandkids. Why have I never seen you there?**

Work, CC had answered after **Wonk** and **Wok** typos, the hand between her legs pumping, the coil of heat in her belly tightening. **You?**

Touché. Let's fix that. I'll be there Friday night, 7PM. So will you.

Yes, ma'am.

Good.

The sign-off had been the final straw. CC had tossed aside her phone and shoved her other hand into her underwear. She'd filled herself with three fingers and stroked her clit with the other hand for all of five seconds before the coil of heat inside her exploded, her back bowing off the bed as she'd come with a matching "Fuck me" groan.

"Carrington got lucky."

CC practically exploded again—from embarrassment. Her cheeks heated to boiling as her gaze shot up into the knowing sets of dark eyes across the tasting room. Black and brown gazes that belonged to her clients—also her friends. After Colby, Jen and Etienne knew her better than anyone in New Orleans, which was why she accepted there was nothing she could do about the blush. She acknowledged it instead with a smirk and raised brow.

"You're gonna *get* lucky," Jen amended, her eyes sparkling with mischief.

CC quirked the other brow.

"Both!" Etienne said with a clap. The deep laugh lines around his eyes crinkled as he hooted with laughter. "Damn, girl."

She closed the text thread, pocketed her phone, then slid off the stool and crossed the room to her friends. Etienne's arms circled her shoulders, Jen's her waist, a good foot of height between the dynamic husband and wife duo.

CC hugged them tight. "It's so good to see you both." She leaned back and took closer stock of her friends. Jen's normally fawn skin was tawny and golden, and the warm undertones of Etienne's brown skin were even more striking than usual. There was only one explanation. "So, which beach did y'all just get back from?"

"Cancun," Jen answered.

"A whole week off," Etienne said. "Glorious."

"While you," Jen said to her, "are pale as a ghost under that blush."

"Half Moon Bay isn't nearly as sunny as Cancun."

"Have you been there for months, Ms. Clarke?" Etienne said as he turned toward the tasting bar. "Because we ain't seen you around these parts since summer."

Cringing, CC grabbed her glass off the table and

downed the last sip of whiskey. Same as with Dram, she had been absent from Tchin Tchin for too long. She'd let work overrun her life again, and Jen and Etienne were among the neglected. She followed them to the bar and claimed the stool next to Jen. "I owe you an apology," she said as she handed her glass to Etienne behind the bar. "I let work get in the way of my life again."

"Well, now we get to be your work too," Jen said. "We'll be seeing a lot of each other over the next month."

"*If* this all goes to plan." Etienne pulled a carton of Jen's favorite iced chicory coffee from the fridge and poured glasses for each of them. "Thank you for jumping on this so quickly," he said as he pushed a glass in front of CC.

She took a sip of the iced coffee, the sweet and bitter blending together perfectly. "Like I would let anyone else handle this deal." She spun so her back was to the bar, allowing her gaze to rove over the space from this angle. "No matter how many times I do this, there's always something special about seeing a client make their dream a reality." She rotated back to her friends. "And seeing that excellence recognized."

"Tchin-tchin," Jen said, lifting her glass for a toast.

Even the distillery's name—Tchin Tchin, both Chinese and French for "Cheers!"—was special for Jen and Etienne, her a third generation Chinese American and him from a Creole family that traced its New Orleans roots to the early 1800s.

"You two were my first real friends in New Orleans and my first clients here," CC said. "You and this place mean something to me. I want to do right by you." She finished her iced coffee and set the glass aside. "Which means we need to talk strategy before the buyer gets here."

For the next half hour, they went over the basic terms Jen and Etienne had already negotiated with Bo Dotson. The CEO of Dotson Brands had tasted Tchin Tchin's award-winning dark rye at a whiskey festival over the summer and had been angling to add Tchin Tchin to the Dotson collection of brands ever since. Purchase price, closing date, and transfer of all but the naming rights had been agreed to in concept. From there, CC probed her clients for where they might land on additional terms that would be negotiated in the deal document. They had just started to discuss the breakup fee in case the deal went sideways when the tasting room's doors opened.

CC recognized Bo Dotson from the hasty bit of research she'd done after getting the call from Jen about the deal. He was, by all accounts, a fair and affable self-made millionaire who wisely invested in real estate for data centers early on. Those assets produced enough income to fund his other venture, Top Hat Wine & Spirits, an impressive collection of fine wines and spirits distributed under his Top Hat label. White, average height, a little soft in the middle but otherwise seemingly fit for a man in his sixties. Just off the golf course too, judging by his shorts, polo, and sunburn. "Well, if it isn't my favorite whiskey team!"

He spoke like he meant it, his grin genuine, the handshakes he gave each of them warm and enthusiastic. The man beside him—Robert Dotson III—was less fervent in his greeting, his gaze only briefly meeting each of theirs before it darted around the space, assessing.

CC would have assessed him further too, but the third member of their party entered, lowering her phone from her ear as she crossed the threshold. Dressed in a three-piece maroon suit, a scarf loosely impersonating a tie and disappearing below her vest and in between the fabulous pair of tits CC couldn't get out of her head, Al looked a world away from the sweater-and-maxi-skirt free spirit of Sunday. But her confidence was unmistakable, as was her bob of wild gray curls, her dark brown eyes that latched onto CC, and the sexy smirk that curled one corner of her painted lips.

"You two know each other?" Etienne asked, catching on.

"Al and I were seatmates on the plane from San Francisco last weekend," CC answered.

"And now I know why getting that drink right was so important to you," Al said before extending her hand to Jen, then Etienne. "Al, short for Annaliese Rosin, counsel for Dotson Brands."

"Nice to meet you," Jen said, then Etienne added, "CC's been with us from the beginning."

"I'm spoiled with my whiskey too," CC said as she bumped Jen's shoulder and smiled in her friends' direction. "They're the best. They've worked hard to build Tchin Tchin, and they deserve to make back everything they've put into it." She swung her gaze back to the Dotsons. "And I don't just mean the dollars. A lot of love went into restoring and outfitting this place." She tipped her head toward the glass wall that ran the length of the tasting room, stacks of barrels behind it.

"And that's exactly why we're interested," Bo said. "We've been searching for a top-shelf whiskey to add to our collection. We believe Tchin Tchin is it." He shifted his earnest gaze to Jen and Etienne. "We'll honor what you've built here."

"You've been acquiring a lot of brands lately," CC said.

Bo shot Al a fond smile. "Because we've got a great closer."

"Our customers expect and deserve the best," Robert added. "We're doing everything we can to bring it to them."

"Tchin Tchin too," Bo said. "By year-end, if you can make it happen. I know Al can on our end."

Jen nodded. "We have confidence CC can make it happen too."

"Terrific!" Bo clapped, his grin wide. "How about a toast?"

Etienne poured a round of shots, and as their clients clinked their glasses together, Al raised hers to CC. If CC had thought her seatmate from the weekend, her date for Friday night, had vanished beneath the designer threads, the sexy confidence in her *I look forward to working with you* made clear two things: that woman hadn't gone anywhere, and this deal was about to get way more complicated.

Chapter Four

CC had intended to swing by home and change into something more Friday-night-out, but by the time she left her firm's Benson Tower office, she had less than fifteen minutes to get to Dram in the Bywater. She pushed through the door of the packed gastropub with less than a minute to spare. She glanced around the immediate vicinity for Al. Not seeing her, CC breathed a sigh of relief. She hated being late. She hung her trench coat on one of the hooks by the door, chuckling at the seasonal-yet-not-for-New-Orleans snowflakes dangling from the rafters, then navigated around the patrons at the host stand and through the pub tables in the center of the dining area.

Reaching the bar was like running a gauntlet, but at least everyone she accidentally bumped into was kind, some even shooting her interested looks. If Tchin Tchin was her favorite distillery in town, Dram was her favorite restaurant. Expressly queer-friendly, the Bywater sensation was full of people like her in a town—hell, country—

where it felt like precious few places were still safe. But at Dram, the word *Haven* was etched in copper in the multicolored stained glass above the door, and that was what it had always felt like to CC. No shame or hiding here, just loud and proud queer folk living their best lives.

The award-winning food and drinks were the cherry on top.

As she neared the bar, CC kept her eyes peeled for Al. Still not seeing her, she diverted to the relatively quiet end of the bar where friends and family stools were tucked near the bar flip. She snagged the one Colby's polka-dot raincoat was draped over and dragged it out of the way of the bar mat where Tony, the head bartender and part owner of Dram, set two drinks for pickup.

He took one look at her and whistled low. "That kind of week?"

She laid her phone on the bar, then gathered up her massive halo of humidity curls into a topknot. "You have no idea."

"You interested in the specials?" He swiped his own black curls off his forehead, his mohawk similarly a humidity-amped riot. "Fireside Rye is back."

She loved Tony's spicy winter concoction, but she needed something stronger tonight. "Vieux Carré."

"Oof, liquor in a water glass. It really has been a week." Tony called for the rolling ladder, then scaled to the top-shelf whiskeys for the Tchin Tchin he knew she preferred.

CC—and at least half the bar—admired Tony's trim hipster body poured into dark jeans, a tight vest, and a light blue dress shirt. While she had no sexual interest in Tony, she could appreciate a fine ass on anyone. And Tony's was one of the finest.

"Stop staring."

CC glanced to the side and found her sister staring too. "You first."

Colby's grin was positively wicked as she pecked CC's cheek. "I don't think I've seen you since Wednesday morning. I heard you come and go on your side of the house, and I heard that godforsaken bullet blender you think makes actual breakfast, but otherwise you've been Casper." They shared a shotgun double a few blocks from Dram. Each had their own space, but they still existed under one roof and shared a large backyard and pool, a major selling point for two women who'd grown up with chilly summers and zero humidity.

"I've been negotiating a letter of intent for a client."

Colby unbuttoned her chef's coat, the polka dots of her dress underneath matching her coat . . . and her Crocs. "Did you get it signed?" she asked as she climbed onto the stool beside her.

"Clients are signing over dinner tonight." Three pages of blood, sweat, and tears. None of the last, really, but plenty of paper cuts and a lot of mental sweat. Al had been a tough negotiator. Tough, but fair. She'd reined in Dotson the Younger's nonmarket terms multiple times. Something about Robert bothered CC—she didn't trust him—but his father seemed genuine. Bo seemed to understand the prize he was getting and wanted to do right by Jen and Etienne. So did CC, which was why she'd been working longer hours than usual.

Tony returned with her drink, plus shots for Colby and himself. A quick toast, then CC took a healthy sip of the spicy smooth cocktail with its herbal twist. She never ordered these outside of New Orleans; they'd never be as good. The French Quarter original went a long way to easing CC down from the stressful work week.

"When's the deal close?" Colby asked.

"December 29," she said, wincing internally.

Colby winced right out in the open. Year-end deals were a fact of life for transactional attorneys. In her fifteen-plus years of practice, CC could count on one hand her deal-free Decembers. Colby had lived through the last five with her. "Why do you do this again?" her sister asked.

"Because I love it."

"Good thing I love you too. Guess I'm flying solo for Hanukkah?"

"Hey, I just did Thanksgiving solo." She tilted her glass toward Colby. "You can handle Hanukkah." Took another sip. "I'm aiming to have this deal buttoned up in time to make Christmas." Theirs was a multifaith family, their father Methodist, their mother Jewish. Usually, the holidays fell close enough that she and Colby could make one quick trip out from New Orleans together. This year, however, Hanukkah fell early in December.

Colby plucked the glass right out of CC's hand and polished off the rest of the cocktail. "That's for being a pain in my ass."

"I'm really sorry."

"I know, babe." Colby kissed her temple before hopping off her stool and rebuttoning her chef's coat. "You want dinner? Greg's doing goulash tonight. It's perfect for this weather."

"Tempting, but I didn't eat lunch until three." Colby opened her mouth to chide her, and CC cut off her well-intentioned lecture. "Whatever you've got for the Sweet Spot will be perfect."

Colby squinted a hazel eye, deciding whether to lecture still, but a shout from the kitchen saved CC's day. Colby let out a frustrated huff, sending a long red wave that had escaped her own topknot fluttering. "Give me ten."

CC was grateful she didn't push. If she had, CC would've had to confess it wasn't exhaustion, but nerves killing her appetite. While she and Al had spoken and exchanged emails countless times the past three days, all those points of contact had been in a purely professional context.

"Will you think me terribly forward if I come right out and ask to take you to bed?"

Purely unprofessional.

CC rotated on her stool, bringing her face to face with the cause of the belly gremlins. "You? No."

"Would you be terribly disappointed if it was just to sleep?" Al smiled, not her usual sexy one, but a tired one that was a mirror of how CC felt right then too.

"Definitely not."

Al set her phone facedown on the bar and clambered onto the stool Colby had vacated, just as easily in today's three-piece twill suit as she had in the maxi skirt and sweater from Sunday. "Opposing counsel put me through the wringer this week."

"And we're just getting started."

"Mama Al!" A muscled arm in chef's whites snaked between them, then around Al's front, engulfing her in a hug. "Where you been?" Greg, the head chef and Tony's husband, gave her cheek a smacking kiss.

Al laughed and leaned into Greg's hold like old friends, like . . . family? CC didn't think she was related to Tony, despite their New York connection, and Greg was born and raised in New Orleans. "Working, Sonoma, working."

"Oh!" Greg—who, in CC's experience, was already an excitable fellow—grew impossibly more excited. "Did you—"

"I did!" From her purse, Al withdrew a jar that she handed to Greg.

He held it to his chest, and for a second, CC was sure he would pet it and call it his precious. "This shit is crack," he said, far more Greg-like.

"What is it?" CC asked.

Al splayed her hands, fingers wide. "The base of that gravy my grandkids covered the walls with."

Greg glanced back and forth between them, as if suddenly catching on to the fact two people he knew were sitting side by side companionably. "I think I interrupted."

CC did the same, glancing between chef and attorney. "And I feel like I walked into a convo in progress, even though I was here first."

Everyone laughed, momentary awkwardness broken.

"We're family," Tony said as he returned to their end of the bar. "Or as near as."

"My son, Tyler, runs Rosin Hospitality," Al explained. "Which is Greg's business partner in this venture."

"And Ty," Greg said, "is married to my best friend's ex-wife."

Facts that did not make CC any less confused. "I think I need a flowchart."

Al was still wiping away the tears from her laugh when Tony placed a Manhattan on the bar for her and a fresh Vieux Carré for CC. "I saw Colby steal most of yours."

"And how do you two know each other?" Greg asked, gesturing between her and Al.

CC's face heated, then heated more when Al shifted on her stool so her leg pressed against hers under the bar. Above the bar, Al swatted Greg's chest, distracting his knowing brown eyes. "We were seatmates on the flight back to New Orleans."

He tipped his head back and laughed, almost as loud as Al just had over CC's flow chart comment. "Half the regulars in this place have been trying to pick up CC since Colby first brought her in here, and you manage it on a plane." He turned his attention to CC. "You know, this one"—he waggled a finger Al's direction—"is trouble."

"Oh, I'm aware." On more than one level.

He laughed again. "This one might give you a run for your money," he said to Al, then tapped the bar with the hand not holding the gravy base. "I'll go check on your dessert," he told CC, then asked Al, "You want anything?"

"Whatever she's having."

Greg leaned across the bar flip, gave his husband a quick kiss, then headed back to the kitchen. Relatively alone again, CC reached for her drink and angled toward Al. "I went straight for dessert. Doesn't mean you have to."

Al nudged her knee higher, spreading CC's thighs farther apart. "Less courses means we get to bed sooner."

"To sleep still?"

The smoldering look in Al's dark eyes made CC wonder. Had her thoughts instead strayed the same heated direction as CC's? Before either of them could say another word, though, Al's phone vibrated on the bar top. She flipped it over; Rob Dotson's name lit up the screen.

CC's rang the next second, Jen's picture on-screen. "Hopefully it's good news."

They spun opposite directions to answer, backs to each other, as the noise in the pub swelled. A large party broke out into "Jingle Bells," the song catching on with other nearby tables too. CC could barely hear her own client, much less Al talking to hers.

Tony appeared across the bar from them and tossed a key ring to Al. "Use the office and wine closet."

"Hold just a second," CC told Jen, then followed Al toward the service area of the restaurant.

Al walked past the wine closet to the office, unlocked it, and gestured for CC to enter. *Two minutes*, she mouthed, then unlocked the next-door wine closet and disappeared inside.

CC closed the office door behind her and lifted the phone back to her ear. "Alright, Jen, I can hear now. What's going on?"

"Do you think we could get something added to the LOI that says the real estate won't be sold separate from the business?"

The unease that had lived at the back of CC's mind the past three days reared its head again. "You think Dotson might?" She crossed the office and leaned a hip against the desk scattered with spiral notebooks and restaurant supply catalogues. "Did they say something to make you think that?" CC had heard nothing of the sort, but other than their meeting Wednesday, her only contact with the Dotsons had been through Al.

"It's not what they said," Jen replied, "so much as what they didn't. All they talk about, especially Rob, is the business, the whiskey, and the operation, but like, in a vacuum, separate from the distillery itself. And their counsel . . ."

CC straightened. "Al?"

"You said she's a real estate attorney."

"The real estate is half the value of the deal. I'd be more concerned if there wasn't a real estate attorney involved. But let me talk to her and see what we can get."

"You think you can reach her now?"

The office door opened, the woman herself entering. "Yeah, should be able to. Give me ten, and I'll get back to you." She hung up and set her phone on the desk while Al closed the door.

She leaned against the back of the closest guest chair facing the desk. "My clients think yours are balking."

"Not balking, just concerned."

"About? You've seen the cash flow and the financing term sheet. You've got contingencies."

CC didn't see the point in hiding the ball. Not when their clients were literally across the table from each other. They'd move forward with this deal tonight or not. "Are your clients planning to sell the land and move the business elsewhere?"

Al's brows raced north. "Why would they?" The surprise in her voice seemed genuine. Either she was a fantastic actress, or this was the first she'd heard about selling the land too. "The current location, that building is ideal for the brand."

"Would they commit to a covenant not to sell?"

Al chuckled as she circled to the front of the chair. "You've been doing this long enough to know that one"— she held up a finger—"they're not going to tie their hands like that, and two"—raised a second one—"this is a letter of intent. Covenants get negotiated in the asset purchase agreement."

All correct. None the answers CC wanted. "A right of first offer, then?" Those were sometimes specified in term sheets.

"Same answer."

Albeit rarely.

She pushed off the desk, meeting Al in the narrow space between them. "Five years ago, I walked into that tasting room, and it was a complete mess. Sections of the roof were missing, the walls shook, and there were critters crawling through the rotted-out floors."

"They've restored it beautifully."

"And their hands and hearts are on every piece of it. We just don't want a bulldozer to come in and—"

The rest of her words were stolen by Al's kiss. By her mouth covering CC's, her tongue tangling with whatever argument CC was making. Obliterating it from her mind. She clasped Al by the jacket lapels and hauled her closer, craving those tits, that body pressed against hers. If they weren't so far from the damn wall, she'd shove Al up against it and pray they didn't make it shake.

Shaking walls.

The deal.

Fuck.

She wrenched their lips apart and staggered back until the backs of her thighs hit the front edge of the desk. "We can't do this."

"Unless you're suddenly going to become incompetent, I don't see how that's possible." Al moved between her spread legs and coasted her hands up CC's thighs, the teasing touch sending heat straight to CC's center. "Competence is such a fucking turn-on."

Regretfully—so, *so* regretfully—CC laid her hands over Al's and stopped their journey toward where she wanted them most. "My competence dictates we can't do this because one"—she tapped the back of Al's right hand—"ethics, and two"—tapped the back of her left one—"I have to trust you and myself that what we're doing is for our clients, not for ourselves. These clients mean something to me, Al."

"And mine don't?"

Al's sharp tone and the sudden jerk of her hands, as if to yank them free, made CC realize how bad that had sounded. She clasped Al's hands before they were gone for good. "I didn't mean it like that. I just . . ." She closed her eyes, took a deep breath, and regathered her words. When she opened her eyes again, Al's dark ones were watching her closely, the lines at the corners deepened. "I have to be able to fight for them and not get distracted by the woman I want to fuck."

Al's expression relaxed, and one corner of her mouth began to hitch. "Well, that's good to hear."

"After we close."

The threatening smirk disappeared, and CC was afraid Al would too, especially once she withdrew her hands. But then Al crossed her arms over her chest, plumping her breasts and exposing the hint of orange lace that matched today's "tie" disappearing beneath the plaid vest. "That's not fair," CC said.

Al flicked a hand at her. "Neither is you all flushed and heaving."

"Pause." She stood, forcing Al to step back and creating some much-needed space between them. "My clients need some assurances on the future use of the land."

"We can negotiate something in the agreement, and if we can't, then your client walks. It's a nonbinding letter of intent."

"After they've held the property for Dotson and spent how many dollars on me and other fees?"

"Dotson came to them, so it's not like the property or assets were on the market. There's no loss there. As for costs, we can agree to a breakup fee." That sounded better, and CC had already talked to Jen and Etienne about their number. But she wasn't above making Al sweat an extra few seconds. "Come on, CC. This is us, as two professionals, ignoring the heaving bosoms of it all."

Her tough negotiator mask cracked, a chuckle sneaking out.

"Our clients are at a dinner table. Let's give them something to celebrate, Red."

CC ignored the wave of desire Al's *Red* sent crashing through her and turned instead. She found a pen among the mess of Tony and Greg's desk, tore off a corner of a catalogue, and wrote the number she was authorized to present to Al.

Who didn't balk at it. Didn't react at all, Al likewise a seasoned negotiator. "Let me make a call."

She ducked out the door and was gone long enough for CC to text Jen that she'd discussed with Al. When she returned, Al was all smiles. "Sounds like we have a deal."

"We have a nonbinding LOI that will hopefully become a deal." She held out her hand. "And then we can fuck."

Al slid a hand into hers, and the spark between their palms turned into a ball of fire. "And then we can fuck."

Chapter Five

The weekend rain let up in time for Al to take her tablet and wine out to the pool for her regular Sunday night call. While summer in New Orleans had been hotter than the face of the sun, the Big Easy's winter was a vast improvement over New York City's version. With the radiant heat from her rental's pool, jeans and a sweatshirt were all she needed to keep her toasty as the stars came out to play above. She had just gotten settled on a lounger with her wine glass in hand and her tablet propped on her knees when the video call from Ezra rang. She accepted the call, and her best friend's handsome face filled the screen.

"Hey, you." Ezra smiled wide, the wrinkles deepening at the corners of his bright blue eyes. "I see you started without me. What are we drinking?"

She snagged the bottle off the side table and held it, label out, in front of her tablet's camera. "Aglianico, 2016 vintage."

Opening bottles from La Montagna Nebbiosa's cellar

had become tradition for their weekly calls. Granted, it was ultimately the responsibility of their winemaker, Archer Scott, to decide which older vintages were released, but she and Ez liked getting their own arms around the inventory of the winery Rosin Hospitality had purchased.

"So, then," Ezra said as he tapped his chin dimple with a finger, pretending to be deep in thought. "It's cool but pleasant there, and you had stew for dinner. Something you made in the slow cooker and can eat all week."

She rolled her eyes at herself. "I gotta start mixing it up."

"We were married thirty-plus years. I know your food and wine habits, and you've been there in New Orleans going on a year now, meaning we've been having these calls for fifty-two weeks now, so I've got the weather and wine pairings down."

"Smart-ass," she said with zero animosity, only a smile for the person who knew her best in the world.

A glass of the same deep garnet wine appeared over Ezra's shoulder, and then so did Noah, Ezra's husband. Noah had been Tyler's childhood best friend, but they'd lost him for thirteen years, Noah on the run from his abusive father. Ezra had happened upon him last fall, all grown up and cheffing at a small-town diner in North Carolina. They'd reconnected, fallen in love, and their family had gotten back a much-missed member.

Ezra took the offered glass and tipped his face up for a kiss. "Thanks, baby."

A quick peck later, Noah shifted his gray gaze to the screen. "Hey, Al."

"Hey yourself. Greg says thank you for the demi-glace."

"Least I could do for the regular crab shipments."

Ezra spun on his stool and pointed out their eat-in kitchen's west-facing windows. "You do know the ocean is right over that hill?"

"You do know the crab that comes out of it is shit?"

Ezra playfully shoved his husband, then lunged sideways, spilling wine over the rim of his glass, as he snagged Noah's belt loop and hauled him back for another kiss. "Seafood snob."

Al laughed, loving their antics, loving seeing her best friend so relaxed and happy. "He is a chef, sweetie, and a damn good one. He's earned the right to be a seafood snob."

"Thank you," Noah said as he ruffled Ezra's curls, then disappeared off-screen. Not far, though, just on the other side of the kitchen island, if Al had to guess by the direction and volume of his voice. "Speaking of, what do we need to plan to make next weekend?"

"Are you all sure? I feel bad asking everyone to schlep here when we were all just together a week ago."

Ezra shook his head. "Don't want to hear it. Tyler has to come out there anyway to visit potential new sites with Greg and Tony." They'd been trying for over a year to open a second Dram location, but Greg's bad luck at launching restaurants had returned with a vengeance. "More importantly, it's Hanukkah. We're celebrating it as a family, and yes, you were just here, but you've been here for every birthday, anniversary, and other major holiday this past year, so this time we're coming to you."

Her chest warmed, both from the wine and from her family's devotion, especially Ezra's. Four years ago, they were ships passing in the night, two overworked professionals, best friends whose sexual needs had diverged but who still loved each other dearly, just differently in their fifties than they had in their twenties. When they'd dissolved their marriage, their friendship could have dissolved too, but they'd fought like hell for their family and for each other. "I love you."

"I love you too." He tipped his glass to her, then took another sip. "And we get to take care of you too. Don't take this the wrong way, but you look like you need it."

She reclined in the lounger and let her eyes drift closed. "Client wants to do one last deal. Year-end sign and close."

A former venture capitalist, Ezra didn't seem the least bit surprised by the tight timeline. He'd been there, done that, been *that* client. "Well, at least Hanukkah falls early this year."

"I'm still planning to make it to Martha's Vineyard for Christmas." While their family was Jewish, their daughter-in-law's, Sloan, wasn't, so their grandkids were being raised multifaith, which meant Christmas with Sloan's family. Not a hardship, as her family included Greg and her ex-husband, Miller Sykes, a Michelin-star chef. "I'm gonna need some of Miller's cooking by then."

Noah's laugh carried over the banging pots and pans. "I won't tell Greg you said that."

She raised her voice for him to hear. "Thank you!" Then lowered it back to normal for Ezra. "How did I become the workaholic?"

"You always were a workaholic. I was just so much worse."

Laughing, they lifted their glasses to that truth. "How's the vineyard?" Running a winery wasn't a cakewalk either, but Ezra had gotten better at delegating, focusing his efforts on the business side and leaving everything to do with the grapes to Archer.

"Good," Ezra said. "Winding down from harvest and starting winter prep. There are groups through each day, but we're not booked solid. More locals and Bay Area folks than tourists."

"Sounds lovely."

"So lovely." Ezra sighed with his whole body. Al didn't think she'd ever seen him so relaxed. Until he wrinkled his nose in a dramatic cringe. "Except for Archer."

"Bored panda?"

"The worst," Noah chimed in as he set a pile of sliced focaccia and a plate of olive oil and balsamic at Ezra's elbow on the island.

Ezra dipped a slice and popped it into his mouth. "No more parade of tourists to fuck."

"Can't he go into San Francisco?" Al asked.

"He could, but he's too attached to the land already. You know how he gets. Dirt under the nails, yada yada."

"There a party close anytime soon?"

"January, Rocky and James's place up here."

"Oh, they're great hosts." She and Ezra had met the

pair over a decade ago at a party in San Francisco. Al had spent a wonderful night bossing around all three men, Rocky a delightful switch who was willing to defer to her Domme. While Ezra was no longer playing in public—he and Noah preferred to keep their kinks private—she and Archer had had some fun with Rocky and James last fall when they'd babysat the vineyard until Ezra had arrived. "They do a good job making everyone feel comfortable."

"Except I'm having to twist Archer's arm to go."

Hmm. She'd never known Archer to turn down an invite to a scene. But Ezra didn't give her time to contemplate, turning that same scrutiny on her. "What about you? Did you contact any of the names on the list I emailed?" He may have been out of the scene himself, but that didn't mean he wasn't still well-connected to the queer and kinky community in their home bases. "Or any leads from Dram or Greg or Tony?"

She sipped her wine and avoided his searching gaze, staring out at the moonlight reflecting on the water of the pool. "I went to several parties in the spring and summer when work was slow, but now that things have picked up again, time's tight."

"Don't become me, Al." A fork scraping across a plate drew her attention back to Ezra, and her stomach growled at the forkful of pasta and mushrooms he lifted to his mouth. "You like sex too much," he said after a bite, "with and in front of others, to cage all that energy up."

"Who says I haven't been having any?"

The fork clattered as it missed the plate and hit the

island. "What's this now?" he mumbled around another bite.

"Have you lost all your manners?" she teased. "And what did Noah fix you to go with the Aglianico?"

Noah circled the island, his own plate in hand, and sat beside Ezra. "Creamy mushroom and leek pasta. Basically an umami bomb."

"Sounds amazing."

"Answer the question, counselor," Ezra said, undeterred.

"Nothing now, except my own hand between my legs."

"They leave town?"

"No, she's the opposing counsel on the deal I'm trying to close."

Noah's cringe mirrored Ezra's. "Ain't that just the luck."

She gulped back the rest of her wine. Nothing lucky about it.

Chapter Six

"Ms. Rosin."

Al turned from the twentieth-floor lobby view of the Superdome to a suited white man standing beside the garlanded reception desk. Midseventies, judging by his deep facial wrinkles, the thinning white hair on his head, and the much bushier white hair of his brows and mustache, the latter yellowed in the center from what Al guessed was decades of smoking. His voice had the gravel of a smoker too. "Welcome to our firm." He crossed the lobby with his hand extended. "I'm Ted Macy."

Of Macy, Rogers & Mitchell, the named partners on the wall behind the reception desk. Al had expected CC to greet her, but after a year practicing in the South, Ted wasn't a surprise. Neither were the next words out of his mouth.

"Will there be anyone joining you from Dotson Brands? Maybe Mr. McDowell or one of the Mr. Dotsons?"

As if her own gray hair and partner title—hell, her own name on the wall of the firm she helped build, Parker Rosin Weeks—weren't enough to prove she could handle this transaction by herself. In this man's estimation, she needed the younger in-house counsel or one of the Dotsons to oversee her work. Over thirty years in practice, and while her name was on the wall somewhere, that glass ceiling was still a long ways up.

She plastered on a fake smile and gave him the truth he couldn't seem to grasp. "Mr. Dotson and his son are working with Kip on our next acquisition. I'm here to close this one."

Deena Arden, the receptionist who'd introduced herself when Al first arrived, pressed her fingers to her lips, holding back the laugh the upturned corners of her mouth betrayed.

Ted, his back to her, remained oblivious. "Of course, our clients are eager to close as well. Let me show you to the war room Ms. Arden set up for the deal." He held an arm out toward the adjacent hallway, but before they could start in that direction, CC emerged from across the lobby. "I can take it from here, Ted."

Al stifled her relieved sigh, ready to be done with Ted and much happier in CC's capable hands.

"Ms. Rosin, this is Ms. Clarke," Ted said, his voice clipped. Al's pent-up sigh became a barely concealed laugh as she imagined how much CC's business casual flair —wide leg, black-and-white houndstooth slacks paired with an even bolder magenta sweater—must rankle boring-suit Ted. "She's the client contact on this case."

Did Ted even know the clients' names? Well, Al did, and CC deserved respect for the job she'd already done. "The attorney who's been with Jen and Etienne from the beginning." She held her hand out, shaking CC's. "Good to see you again."

"You two have met before?" Ted said.

"Last week," Al replied. "CC was a helluva negotiator on the LOI. I've been in this business thirty years, and I'd hire her in a hot minute."

Huffing, he straightened and buttoned his suit coat. "Well, I'm happy to help," he said, chin lifted, voice snotty and rude in that Southern way that still came off as polite. It impressed Al as much as it pissed her off. The New Yorker in her could never pull it off. "In case you ladies need someone else's eyes on anything."

Someone, as in a man's, in case their womanly eyes weren't enough. "Thank you, Ted," Al said. "We'll keep you in mind."

He didn't miss the brush-off, which only made his retreat more epic. Once he turned the corner, Deena finally let loose the snicker she'd been fighting. CC split an amused smirk between the two of them. "Behave, both of you."

"It's not every day someone calls him on his shit." Deena swung her green gaze from CC to Al. "I owe you a coffee for that."

"Nope, I owe *you* a coffee for setting up our war room."

"I like her," Deena said to CC. "You better watch it, Carrington, or someone's gonna steal your crown."

Laughing, CC pretended to adjust one on her head. "Still fits."

Al waited until they were on their way down the hallway to ask what *the crown* was about.

"Staff favorite," she said, then lowered her voice. "Not that it's too hard around here. Ted's not even the worst."

Al believed it; she'd seen worse. "Second firm I worked at, one of the senior partners used to put his papers on the floor so all the women had to bend over to pick them up."

CC made a disgusted noise in the back of her throat. "There's one partner here who tells me I'll make partner because I 'never got knocked up,' while the one woman partner we have tells me I'll never make partner because I 'lack maternal instincts.'"

"Zevel," Al cursed.

"There's that too, never mind my dad's Methodist."

"Have you thought about leaving? Or telling someone?"

She didn't answer right away, a more telling reply than anything she could say. Before Al could nose further, a young Black woman appeared at the door to the conference room at the end of the hallway. She was as tall as CC, also smartly dressed, and her dark hair was clipped short, highlighting her big brown eyes and the sharp lines of her face. "All ready for you, CC."

Her familiar nasal drawl was a pleasant surprise. "I recognize that accent," Al said with a smile.

"Al, this is Brynn Cary, originally from the Bronx, graduated Tulane Law and joined MRM earlier this fall after spending the last two summers with us. Brynn, this is

Annaliese Rosin, Dotson's lead counsel on the Tchin Tchin deal."

"Al, please." She shook Brynn's hand, then followed her and CC into the conference room. "How's practice treating you so far?"

"Never a dull moment," Brynn replied.

"And there won't be any on this case either," CC said.

Starting with a mountain of file boxes, apparently. "Fucking hell," Al cursed. "What's with all the paper? I thought I saw an e-room invite come through over the weekend."

"We did set up an e-room for what we have digitally, but that building is from the 1800s."

Al recalled the bronze plaque at the front entrance of the tasting room and answered her own question. "Old records."

"We're digitizing more each day," Brynn said, "but it takes time."

"We didn't want to delay getting started on due diligence," CC added. "And honest to God, sometimes it's easier to read 1800s chicken scratch on paper than on screen."

She wasn't wrong. "Fair enough."

"I want to get back to the asset purchase agreement so you have a draft to look at by midweek. Can I leave you with Brynn? She'll go over how we've organized everything in here and in the e-room, including our checklist and workflow."

"By all means."

"Excellent." CC started toward the door. "Deena will

have lunch brought in around noon. You can let me know then if anything is missing that you'll need."

Al cut a smirk in CC's direction. "Two things on my list already."

She rolled her eyes. "Brynn, watch out for this one."

"Yeah, no," Brynn said with a knowing smile. "I'm not getting caught between whatever fire you two"—she gestured between them— "got going already."

"What?" Al gasped in mock offense, hand splayed over her chest. "I was just gonna say what you need is a menorah in that window"—she pointed at one, then the other—"and a Christmas tree in that one. We need some holiday spirit in here."

"I'll get right on that." CC chuckled on the way out of the room, her husky laugh stoking the embers of a fire that still smoldered from a week ago. One Al had to ignore for the time being. All the more reason to get this deal closed sooner rather than later.

She turned to Brynn. "All right, show me what you got."

Chapter Seven

"We've got a problem."

Minimizing the revised asset purchase agreement Al had revised, CC rotated her chair toward the destroyer of documents herself. At some point between this morning when Al had dropped off a French Truck coffee and now, she had ditched her navy velvet blazer, rolled up her silk dress sleeves, and donned a pair of glasses. It was a look, including the binder clips holding up her sleeves, that worked for CC. She rested back in her chair, rocking slightly as she crossed her legs. "And I've got a problem with most of your revisions to the APA."

"That's why *we* negotiate." Al dropped into the visitor chair. "Not one of our problems."

"*Problems*, as in plural."

She winked. "Was softening you up."

"I have a question first." One that had intrigued her for the better part of a week. "How did a real estate lawyer become Dotson's go-to closer on their whiskey deals?" No one person's journey in the legal profession was exactly the same, and CC was particularly interested in those that took interesting twists and turns. Perhaps because her own had swerved so unexpectedly too, and she was still trying to find a road that felt right.

Al relaxed in her chair, kicked off her shoes, and drew a knee up, like they were having a casual conversation on the couch instead of in the office. "Bo's been with me since he started investing in data centers. I do all the joint venture and real estate work for those. That's been . . ." She paused, as if mentally counting. "Over fifteen years. Working together that long, he learned about my family's hospitality and venture capital connections."

The winding road was making more sense now. "And Dotson wanted to use those connections."

"They wanted someone who could speak their language across all their investments."

"Impressive."

"I could say the same about you. You're a food and beverage lawyer with her hands in real estate and corporate law."

Her cheeks heated, but she didn't lower her chin or divert her gaze, not shunning the spotlight on the rare occasion it was given. "It's virtually impossible to separate them, especially in New Orleans."

"Also makes you versatile and keeps your options open."

"That too." MRM wasn't an ideal fit, but there hadn't been a lot of options six years ago for an attorney who'd had to restart in a new town with virtually no connections.

She was just starting to feel like she had a solid book of business and was wary about risking it solo or giving it up to go in-house. MRM, as a firm, had a solid reputation, decent infrastructure, great support staff, and associates like Brynn who would make a difference one day.

"You're good, CC." Al's compliment drew her back to the present. "I may have bled all over your draft APA, but that's tactics. You do good work for your clients."

"Thank you." She leaned forward, forearms on the desk, taking the opening to get them back on track before she was as bright red as the sweater she'd grabbed out of the closet that morning. "But my clients have problems, plural, it sounds like."

"Easy, medium, or hard?"

That didn't sound good. "Give me the medium."

"Rail lines. You got a copy of the survey in here?"

"Yep." CC rose from her desk, retrieved the survey from the stack of rolls in the corner, and unfurled the over-size paper on the round table tucked into the windowed corner of her office.

Al stood beside her, leaning over the survey and pointing at the unused spurs that ran across the back corner of Tchin Tchin's lot. "Title company is refusing to insure over these this time."

"If this is medium, I fear hard." Chasing down anything from rail companies was a bitch. "And how is this only medium?"

"Because I have a contact whose entire job is to chase down easement releases. Will cost the sellers, though."

CC righted herself and leaned a hip against the table.

"Why does the buyer need this? Those lines are a relic at the back of the property. It's not like the rail company is going to resume use, they don't interfere with access, and there's no encroachment by the Tchin Tchin building or any neighboring building."

Al mirrored her posture, arms crossed. "Keeping our options open for future expansion."

Last week's sliver of worry returned—not yet a full-blown wave, but an undertow nipping at her heels. What exactly were the Dotsons going to do with this property?

Before she could press, Al carried on. "You didn't let Jen and Etienne close without coverage when they bought the property. We'd take the title coverage if they'd give it, but they won't."

"Fine, get the release." It would be a costly hassle, but one that would serve everyone's interest in the long run. "Okay, what's the hard problem?"

"Your specialty. Transfer of the liquor license."

CC left the survey on the table and returned to her desk chair. "We already started the paperwork."

"Yes," Al said as she reclaimed the guest chair. "But we need wiggle room on the capacity."

The undertow grew stronger. She'd been in New Orleans long enough to be wary of a brewing riptide. "To go with your expanded facility?"

"Hence the hard part. You got a contact?"

"Y'all don't?" This wasn't the first whiskey brand Dotson had purchased.

"Our contact is in enterprise distribution. This will be the first tasting room Dotson is operating."

"So they intend to keep it?"

Al eyed CC curiously, like she'd suddenly grown a third head. "Of course they intend to keep it. They want to expand production and distribution, but with a high-end product like Tchin Tchin, Bo intends to show it off. This is what he's been after for some time." She curled her fingers in air quotes and hilariously imitated her client's Southern drawl. "Completes the collection."

The undertow eased, the riptide threat passing. "I'll make a call," CC said before rotating toward her computer and maximizing Al's revised APA. "Which brings us back to your bloodletting."

Al chuckled as she leaned back and folded her hands over her middle. "We'll get there, but that's not the easy problem." Her dark eyes sparkled, that mischievous glint CC remembered from the airport and from Dram the other night begging the question.

"All right," CC said. "I'll bite. What's easy?"

"I'm hosting first night dinner for Hanukkah on Thursday night, and I have no idea where to find everything I need."

"Like what?"

"A menorah, to start."

"You didn't bring one?"

"Everything we didn't sell went to the winery in Sonoma."

She cut Al an exaggerated frown. "Well, that was poor planning."

"Not gonna argue."

Chuckling, CC opened her web browser and the tab

with the online order she'd already started. "I'll add another menorah to my cart to go with the one for the conference room. I can tell you where to find the rest if you give me a list."

"Or you could show me."

"Al—"

"As a friend and colleague." She leaned forward and braced her forearms on her crossed knees. "And as someone you might trust with more in the future."

The idea had merit. While they'd agreed to no sex until the deal closed, their agreement didn't prevent them from spending time together, from getting to know each other better outside of work. Even if nothing more developed postdeal, she'd make a friend, which was hard to do as an adult, especially one who worked as much as CC. A friend who worked just as hard and who would understand if she needed to cancel on a dime. And if something more did develop postclosing, if it included the kind of sex CC needed, she would need that trust to be there with Al.

"All right, I'm in," she said. "But when are we going to have time for this shopping spree?"

"Tomorrow night, assuming we get medium and hard taken care of."

"And a draft APA out to our clients."

Al righted herself in the chair and scooted closer. "Deal."

Chapter Eight

"Hard's done." CC slapped a piece of paper down on top of the title commitment Al was reviewing. "Or as much of it as I can do."

Al scanned the notice of public hearing for her client's expanded liquor license. December 19, preclosing. "That'll work." She grabbed her phone and fired off a calendar invite to the Dotson folks who would need to attend.

As she typed, CC spun out the adjacent conference room chair and plopped into it, still graceful despite her way-past-quitting-time slouch. "Have you been through these hearings before?"

"Not here." Al removed her reading glasses, tossed them onto the table, and rubbed her tired eyes. The past week of squinting over ancient documents was catching up with her. She'd happily take a break from title hell to prepare for a zoning hearing. "I've handled plenty of others, though, and we had to get a variance for the winery last year."

"You're barred in California too?"

"Hell no. Couldn't waive into that one." She drew a knee up, propping the heel of her bare foot on the edge of her seat. "I had a local counsel assist, a specialist from the firm my daughter-in-law, Sloan, works at in San Francisco."

"But you handled the rest of the transaction?"

Al nodded. She had an idea where this line of questioning was headed. The inevitable place it went with most folks who were new to her circle of familial chaos.

"And it works? For real?" CC asked. "You still being best friends and business partners with your ex?"

Exactly where Al had anticipated. "You're skeptical," she said with a chuckle.

"I had to leave California because of mine."

Al's laughter died. "I'm sorry, I didn't—"

CC waved off her apology. "Ancient news."

Except Al didn't think that it was. She suspected that history—whatever it was—probably had something to do with CC being slow to trust now. Al would have to earn more of her trust before she'd get the whole story. Al's story, on the other hand, was an open book. "Ezra and I met at a frat party freshman year, and then we met at a different kind of party. The sort my parents had disowned me for. The kind of trust Ezra and I built over three decades doesn't just go away, not when neither of us did anything to violate the other's. I want what's best for him, he wants what's best for me, and for both of us that was to go our separate ways romantically. But in other aspects of our lives, he's still my partner, and we both want what's best for our kids and grandkids."

CC remained quiet for several long seconds, the squeaking swivel of her chair the only sound in the room. Then, seeming to reach acceptance, she smiled the soft shy grin that made Al's heart race. "Like Hanukkah all together here?"

"I'm not sure that's what's best for any of the adults, but there you have it." Al spread her fingers wide, a gravy reminder, and CC laughed, full-throated and enticing.

Would a little flirtation here be a push too far for CC? She kept her gaze locked with the one across from her, watching for any hesitation. Seeing none, seeing that warm brown heat, Al began to scoot her chair closer.

Only to be interrupted by a knock on the conference room door. "Getting late, isn't it?" Ted said. He leaned his tall, spindly frame against the doorjamb and turned a pack of cigarettes end over end in his hand. "No one at home waiting for his supper?"

"We're just hammering out some title issues," CC said, politely ignoring Ted's heteronormative misogyny.

"I bet I could make quick work of that," he offered.

"We're good," Al said, eschewing polite for getting rid of this asshole as quickly as possible. "And when we're done, my personal chef will have dinner waiting for us."

"Oh." He pushed off the door and tucked his smokes away. "You're having dinner together?"

Al couldn't tell if he was suspicious or judgmental, or both. In any event, she was reckless enough to poke the bear. Might as well get it all out on the table. "Least I could do for CC showing me where to find what I need for my family's Hanukkah celebration."

Ted's nose wrinkled, and he pressed his lips together, yellowed mustache bushy enough to tickle the bottom one. "Then I don't suppose you'll want an invitation to the firm's Christmas party?"

"I would love one," she replied enthusiastically. And then continued to fuck with this man's preconceived notions enthusiastically. "Assuming I'm not in Cape Cod celebrating Christmas with our daughter-in-law's family."

CC, who had apparently lived in the South long enough to learn the fake polite skill, spared Ted further confusion. "I'll make sure she has the date."

"Fine," he huffed, then turned on his heel and bolted. They waited for his footsteps to fade around the corner before devolving into a fit of snickers.

Victorious, Al propped an elbow on the table, chin in hand, and grinned. "He's so confused."

"Personal chef?"

"Greg Valteau, of course, who"—she checked the time on her phone—"will have a table waiting for us in an hour. We better get going."

"What about the asset purchase agreement?"

She stood, slid her feet back into her heels, and offered a hand up to CC. "Already reviewed and sent to my clients." CC opened her mouth, and Al, anticipating her next question, continued. "And the rail company's in-house counsel just has to review and sign off on the quit-claim deed the consultant got in front of him this afternoon." She squeezed CC's hand still in hers. "So, how about that shopping spree, Red?"

Chapter Nine

"I'm glad we shopped first." Al folded her hands over her stuffed belly. "I will not be functional for the next six hours."

"Make that seven." Colby appeared beside their table, two plates in hand. She lowered the first in front of her sister. On it was a fluffy open-faced biscuit slathered in what looked and smelled like apple butter. It was topped with a mountain of whipped cream and an artful swirl of deep red coulis—cranberry, if Al had to guess. "Today's Sweet Spot for you."

CC's grin was so wide, so fond that it was all Al could do not to grab her phone and snap a picture. Or to glide the foot resting against CC's under the table higher. Al was seriously considering the latter when Colby placed the second plate in front of her. "And cranberry apple sufganiyot for you."

All thoughts of tempting CC momentarily fled, replaced by her own giddy delight. The doughnuts were fluffy, lightly powdered, and oozing jelly. Joy on a plate, one of Al's favorite foods of the holiday season. And fuck if they didn't taste as good as they looked. She was so lost in the sweet, tart, fried batter thrill that she didn't even notice Colby rummaging through their bags until CC untangled their feet so she could nudge her sister.

"Manners, Col," she lightly chided.

"Since when?"

"It's fine." Al plucked the second doughnut off her plate. "I have grandchildren who rummage through everything."

"Yes," CC said, "but they are children."

"Ooh!" Colby held up one of the two stained glass dreidels Al and CC had found at a funky little shop just around the corner. "This is gorgeous."

"CC picked it out," Al said. "Check out the menorah she found too."

Colby nosed around in the bags some more until she uncovered the spinning menorah, a wheel of rainbow colors, each with a candle holder.

Colby's wide eyes swung to her sister. "Please tell me you bought one of these for our place."

"Of course I did."

She planted a smacking kiss on CC's cheek, transferring her bright red lipstick in a stamp-worthy smudge. "I love you."

"Ugh, I love you too." CC wiped at her cheek, but the affection in her words belied the exaggerated annoyance. "Are you packed?"

"Yep, before I came to work." Colby rewrapped the

goods and placed them carefully back in Al's bag. "Cab is picking me up at fuck-off early."

CC chuckled around a bite. "I'll take you."

"And then you'll go to French Truck and work all day."

Al lowered the last bite of her doughnut. "You're not going home too?" she asked CC.

"We traded," Colby answered. "She took Thanksgiving, I took Hanukkah."

"And we're both going at Christmas," CC said. "If we" —she gestured with her fork between herself and Al—"get the deal mostly wrapped by then."

"I'm not doing two alone, so you better," Colby said, then skirted out of reach before CC could swat her with her napkin.

"You two are exactly like I imagined," Al said with a laugh.

"How so?"

"She tests you, and you adore her. Reminds me of how Tyler and Noah were growing up. Definitely how Molly and Michael are already."

CC nodded as she finished her last bite, then wiped her hands. "Colby's the one who lured me down here. If she hadn't, I don't know where I'd be."

"With that bit of delicious"—Al pointed at the plate CC had just wiped clean—"of course you came with her."

CC traded her napkin for her coffee. "She's been making these for me since I was a kid, though back then it was Smucker's and Cool Whip. But she's been baking biscuits since she could reach the dials on the oven. Now the jelly changes with the season, even more so here, and sometimes she flavors the whipped cream, but the biscuit is still the best part."

Al popped in the last bite of her doughnut and hummed happily. "She's truly magic with baked goods."

CC's sexy laughter was cut short by a ding on Al's phone. She wiped her own hands and flipped the device, reading the text on-screen. "We'll have the quitclaim deed for the rail tracks in the morning."

CC lifted her mug. "And that's medium done. Thank you."

Al clinked her own cup against CC's. "I know exactly how to celebrate."

CC slumped in her chair and waved a hand, palm out in surrender, groaning dramatically. "There's no more room."

"Not tonight, silly." She slid her foot back against CC's under the table. "Tomorrow night. Join us for Hanukkah."

"You don't have—"

"I know I don't have to, but I want to. It's a day for family and lights." She glided her foot that little bit higher she'd wanted to earlier, notching it behind CC's calf. "And you're one hell of a firecracker, Red."

Chapter Ten

They were barely outside Dram's backdoor when Colby launched into her interrogation. "Okay, spill."

CC had expected as much but had hoped—against all odds—that maybe Colby would wait until they made it the three blocks home.

No such luck. "That's twice now you and Al have been at Dram together," Colby continued as she tugged a wagon full of baking supplies behind her. "And both times you've been flirting up a storm."

"She's the opposing counsel on the year-end deal I'm working," CC said, addressing the first part of her sister's question.

Colby wasn't letting her skip the second. "Yes, and I've lived with you for six years while you've been practicing and you've never looked like this"—she made a sweeping gesture in front of CC's face—"over a deal."

CC continued her evasive maneuvers. "What all did you put in that wagon?"

"Everything I need to make babka, challah rolls, dreidel cookies, and more sufganiyot."

She was stress baking, like she always did before a long flight. Colby loved to travel—she'd been all over the world—but she was a nervous flyer. She coped by staying up and baking the entire night before so she'd pass out as soon as the plane hit cruising altitude. But this was extreme, even for Colby. "Are you planning to take some home because I can't eat that many doughnuts?"

Colby shot her a do-you-need-more-coffee glare. "One, yes, you totally can, and two, it's for you to take to Al's tomorrow."

"How—"

"I heard her tell Tony to add one."

"I was thinking of skipping out."

Colby shook her head hard enough to dislodge the rest of her flagging topknot. "Nope. You like her, she likes you, and I don't want you to spend First Night alone."

"I'll be fine."

"I know. Al is fucking hot."

"Colby!"

She shrugged and flicked her hair out of her face. "I'm not wrong."

CC didn't see a way out of this convo; Colby was relentless. And maybe she needed to have it anyway, to work out where she was with things in her own head, where things might go with Al and if she was okay with that. Colby was the only person who knew her entire story, what it would mean for CC to put herself out there again. "You're not wrong," she admitted.

"She strikes me as the Domme type too."

"You're not wrong there either."

"Ooh, score for you, sis!"

"She's another attorney, Col. After San Francisco . . ." Her words died as they turned the corner onto their street, as she remembered another much hillier street where hope had died a swift and fiery death. "I can't start over, not again. I don't have another bar exam in me."

Colby snorted. "Not sure I would survive another one either." They both laughed, but it was half-hearted, tinged with sadness and shared commiseration. Colby only spoke again once they reached their house. "You have to do what feels right, CC, but if you do pursue something, I don't think it'll be like last time. I've been working at Dram for a while now, with Al's family, and they're good people. She seems like good people too. She doesn't seem like an immature, power-hungry, shitty Domme."

CC both winced and laughed at the succinct, too accurate description of her ex. And she tended to agree. Al was mature, successful, and completely at ease in her skin, nothing like Quinn. But that wasn't the only concern CC had when it came to a possible postdeal relationship with Al. And that was what it would need to be: a relationship, not just the occasional hookup. CC didn't do casual; she knew that about herself and wasn't about to lie and say otherwise for even the best lay. "I don't even know how long she's in NOLA for. Her family is in California."

"Well," Colby said as they climbed the couple of steps, carrying the cart, "you are barred there. Isn't that convenient?"

"I have no intention of leaving here or you." CC waited while Colby unlocked the door to her side of the house, then rolled the cart in behind her. "In any event, nothing can happen until after we close this deal. I can't compromise this for my clients." CC closed and locked the door, only to be bear-hugged by her sister.

"You're a good attorney, sis. And a good sister and friend."

She rested her head against her sister's temple. "And I will take you to the airport at fuck-off early because I love you, but I will not make it there and back safely if I stay up all night with you baking."

"Just snore from the couch and keep me company?"

CC returned Colby's cheek-smacking kiss from earlier. "I can do that."

Chapter Eleven

CC stood on the sidewalk in front of a gorgeous two-story Irish Channel home, its siding painted seafoam green, its trim and balconies white, and the front door a bright canary yellow. Lights shone from the floor-to-ceiling windows, a string of metallic letters spelling out *CHAG SAMEACH!* stretched across the upstairs balcony, and a matching wreath of blue, silver, and gold was hung on the front door.

Said door swung open, and CC had to do a double take. If it weren't for the mohawk of black curls and the familiar smile, she might not have recognized Tony in cargo shorts and a tee instead of his usual behind-the-bar jeans, vest, and starched shirt.

"Hey, CC." He jogged down the front steps and joined her on the sidewalk. "Let me help you with that." Bending, he lifted one end of the cart full of baked goods while CC picked up the other, the two of them carefully navigating the brick steps.

"Colby went a little overboard," she said.

"You should see the pastry freezer at Dram."

Inside, they lowered the cart and CC shut the door behind them. "She loves to travel but hates flying, so she works herself into a frenzy the night before she leaves. Helps her sleep on the plane."

"As much as we wouldn't want to lose her, there are plenty of gigs for a talent like hers in SF."

CC laughed out loud. "She would never live that close to our parents again."

Tony's answering laugh was drowned out by a wave of noise from the back of the house—banging pots, a pressure cooker whistle, more laughter—all of it echoing down the long narrow hallway. Typical double gallery side hall floor plan for this neighborhood, and no surprise this bunch of foodies would be gathered in the kitchen and living areas at the back. And with the enticing aromas drifting from that direction—brisket, onions, fried potatoes—no one could fault them.

She and Tony were halfway down the hall when a mini commotion reached them first. Amos, Tony and Greg's son who CC recognized from around Dram, was careening in their direction, two other kids on his heels, both of them freckled gingers.

Arms spread, Tony stepped in their path. "Slow down before someone gets hurt."

Likely the smallest one. The little boy couldn't have been more than three, and he was struggling to keep up with Amos and the redheaded girl, his sister if CC had to guess.

"Say hello to CC," Tony said to Amos. "And introduce your cousins."

"Hey, CC." Amos waved, then elbowed the girl at his side. "This is Molly."

She elbowed him right back, then jutted her thumb over her shoulder. "That my brother, Michael."

CC smiled to cover her awkwardness, unsure if she should bend down and make conversation or maybe offer the kids something from Colby's cart. She'd babysat the neighbor's kids once as a teen and known right then that she'd never have children of her own. Decades later, she still didn't know how to relate to them. But as with most kids, Amos and the redheads weren't that interested in her either. Another quick round of waves and they skirted around Tony and into the room to their left where a blanket fort was pitched between two twin beds, Legos scattered on the floor beneath it.

"Don't take it personally," Tony said as they started down the hallway again. "They're always like this when they see each other. In their own world, no adults allowed."

"Colby and I were the same with our cousins whenever we—" They emerged from the hall, through a wet bar she would have drooled over if she weren't too busy drooling over the kitchen spread out before her. She and Colby had upgraded their own kitchens when they'd bought their place, but this was next level.

"Dessert is here," she vaguely heard Tony say, and barely registered Greg throwing her a wink and a "You know she is." She was still too caught up trying to take in the kitchen of her and Colby's dreams. A massive cooking and serving island stretched the length of the space, and on either side were wide aisles, an artfully set banquet dining table to the right, and three massive chefs to the left, including Greg, operating between the sixty-inch range top on the island and the double sinks and prep space beneath the wall of windows.

"Miller Sykes," Tony said, and the chef in plaid flipping latkes in a skillet on the range raised a hand. "Noah Rosin," he said next, and the one chopping fennel who had more hair on his chin than on his head raised his hand. "This is CC, Colby's sister."

"Oh!" Miller flashed her a grin, wide and bright in his gray and chestnut scruff. "So you're the person I need to convince to move to Boston." Except Chef Plaid sounded way more Southern than Bostonian, and what did he mean move there?

Before she could voice her confusion, Greg flicked him with latke batter. "I'm not letting you have Colby. Not when *Eater* goes on for paragraphs about how good our desserts are now."

Have Colby?

"Give up, y'all," Noah said, the *y'all* at odds with the New York accent. He tossed the chopped fennel in a large bowl, added what looked like grapefruit pieces, then went to town with a pepper mill. "She's from California. I win."

"Oh, shut up, Mister Lives on a Vineyard." Miller flicked batter on down the line. "Unfair advantage."

"Times two!" Greg agreed, but then said to Miller, "Though in fairness, you used to live there too."

More batter flew, and CC's head spun just as fast,

struggling to keep up with the rapid-fire banter, the choreographed kitchen operation, the mentions of moving, and chefs fighting over Colby. It was a storm she hadn't been prepared for, and it was tilting her world off-balance.

Until a familiar laugh from the far end of the room on the other side of Chef Mountain focused her attention.

She stepped right, out from the end of the island, and the rest of the living area came into view. Past the kitchen and the fireplace that divided the back wall of the house in half was a cozy space filled with two oversize chairs angled at either end of a corner sectional and a giant ottoman-slash-coffee-table. All the furniture—and the people on it—faced the kitchen, including the casual version of Al who CC had first met at SFO. Her maxi skirt tonight was navy with gold starbursts, her sweater a matching dark blue, and her bare feet poked out from under the hem of the skirt. She looked relaxed and happy, tucked under the arm of a strikingly attractive older man with copper and silver curls. They were totally caught up in whatever the redheaded woman on the arm of the chair to their right was saying. In said chair sat a ginger man, and for perhaps the first time in her life, CC thought maybe her own red hair was in the majority tonight. It was the only thing that remotely made her feel like she belonged here.

Tony rejoined her, glass in hand. "Manhattan for you," he said, handing her the cocktail. "It's a lot, I know. Let's leave Larry, Moe, and Curly to it."

That earned him a flick of latke batter, then like the children in the hall, the chefs quickly forgot they existed, arguing who was which Stooge. She and Tony continued on toward the living area, Al finally glancing their way just as they cleared the end of the island. Her bright smile made CC's pulse pound, and her dark eyes, filling with that same smoldering heat from their first encounter, made all of CC's pumping blood race a different direction. Neon Danger signs blinked in her head, and yet CC didn't turn and run, too intrigued by this woman and her unconventional family.

"Someone's husbands are misbehaving," Tony said.

"Including yours?" Ezra, CC assumed, given his age and accent and the easy affection between him and Al.

"Of course," Tony replied. "Which is why I'm here with this beautiful lady."

Smiling, Al unfolded from the couch and stepped around Ezra's knees. "They're as much trouble together as the kids." She crossed to CC's side and looped an arm through her free one. "This one's trouble too, so watch out. Everyone, this is CC, Colby's sister. She's also across from me on a deal at the moment."

"My condolences," Ezra said as he stood. Al swatted his stomach, and he gasped in mock outrage. "What? You're the best." He extended a hand to CC. "Ezra Rosin, forever her number one fan."

"CC," she said, returning the shake. "Nice to meet you."

"These are our kids," Ezra carried on, gesturing first to the pair of redheads in the one chair. "Our son, Tyler, and his wife, Sloan."

"The two little redheads running around are ours,"

Sloan added, the same trace of Southern in her voice as in Miller's.

"The gravy monsters from Thanksgiving," Al said before she ruffled the brown hair of the younger man in the closest chair. His arms were full of strawberry blond baby. "And this is Miller's husband, Clancy, and their daughter, Holland."

CC stepped closer so Clancy wouldn't have to stand or reach far to shake her hand. "You two have a connection there? To Holland?" she asked Clancy.

He laughed. "No. It was Sloan's idea. None of our husbands can make a hollandaise that doesn't break."

"And that one"—Sloan nodded to the bundle in Clancy's arms—"is sure to break them all. I thought it was funny."

So did CC, especially as an argument broke out behind them, Miller and Greg debating what sauce to serve with the brisket.

Clancy rose and adjusted Holland in his arms. "I'm going to go break that up since our window to eat is quickly closing. She's got maybe forty-five minutes left on this nap."

"Give her to me," Al said, arms out, careful not to wake the baby as Clancy gently handed her over. CC shifted on her feet, giving them more room, which only served to draw Al's attention. "Do you want to hold her?"

CC shook her head. "I'm not a natural."

"That's fine." Al's smile didn't falter, a pleasant change from the judgment CC often received for the truth. Al bent and kissed the baby's forehead. "I'll keep her all to myself."

Ezra lowered his voice, whispering, "You always were a sucker for a redhead."

CC sipped her drink and took another step back. She braced herself on the arm of Clancy's vacated chair, the earlier storm winds kicking up again and tipping her off-balance, her earlier intrigue veering more toward wariness. She liked this family. Colby was right. They seemed like good people—warm, open, and accepting—but they were tight. Tighter than most she'd experienced. They had their own rhythms and language and a world in common. It felt a bit like that time she and Colby visited the French village that made Col's favorite cheese. CC couldn't understand a word or thing going on around her and had felt lost all afternoon. And she was rarely lost with a plate of cheese in front of her. Maybe she should have asked Colby for a crash course on the Rosins last night instead of falling asleep on the couch. Could Col spare five minutes to give her one now? Her flight had landed a couple hours ago, and dinner was still a few hours away there.

She tipped back the rest of the drink, then set the glass on the end of the island. "I'm going to go call Colby," she told Al. "Make sure she got home."

"Use my office," Al said. "Less chance of arguing chefs or gravy monsters."

Sloan pushed off the arm of the other chair. "I'll show you the way." She opened the patio door off the living room, led CC down a short set of steps and around the steaming in-ground pool, to the structure at the back of the lot. "The owner flipped it so the other side is the garage," Sloan explained as she pulled open the black-framed accordion doors where garage doors clearly used to be. "Made this a pool house that Al uses as her office."

CC's gaze roamed over the space. A comfy-looking chaise lounge and minimalist table and office chair for furniture. White walls like the rest of the house, another marble-top wet bar, a flat-screen television over it, bookshelves along the other wall, a large black-and-white framed photograph of a rainy Central Park on the opposite one.

"You okay?" Sloan asked behind her.

CC turned from the framed photograph. "Yeah, of course."

Sloan leaned against the doorjamb. She was around Al's height, probably around CC's age, with long red barrel curls and blue eyes that sparkled with even more mischief than Al's. If there was a chief troublemaker in this family, Sloan was probably that person. "It's a lot when you first get pulled into their orbit. Miller and Greg and I were our own island for years until we met Tyler and got pulled in. Hang tight. It's worth it, I promise."

"Al and I are just work friends."

"Sure," Sloan drawled. Definitely Southern. "Ask Tony how that went." She turned on her heel and threw a wink over her shoulder. "And you're totally Al's type."

Chapter Twelve

When the chefs finally gave the ten-minute warning and CC still hadn't returned from the office, Al handed Holland off to Ezra and went looking for her missing guest. Earlier, CC had looked like a deer caught in the headlights, too many moving pieces to process. Maybe throwing her right into the frying pan wasn't the best idea. At the same time, there was no use hiding the ball. If anything were to develop postclosing between them, CC needed to know Al came with a big family full of love and chaos. She needed to be okay with ex-spouses who still loved each other, with family that transcended blood, and with a mix of people and cultures that usually worked well together but did also occasionally butt heads. Though any argument always ended in laughter.

Al found CC still in the office surveying the various plaques and framed photos on the bookcases. Al looked her fill a minute—CC was stunning tonight in dark jeans, a gold cowl-neck sweater, and ascot-style boots that laced up the back of her calves—before asking, "You freaking out yet?"

"How'd you guess?" She turned from the shelf, and while the deer in headlights look was gone, a different one Al liked even less had settled in her brown gaze.

"Did you get in touch with Colby?"

"I told her Miller Sykes was making latkes in your kitchen, and she made honking geese noises." She circled the desk and rested back against the front edge. "You know, I looked you up once I had your full name, but I didn't know you were this well-connected. Col filled me in." Her gaze flicked over Al's shoulder to the house. "Didn't know you were this wealthy either."

"It's a rental," Al said. "But if I wanted to buy it, I could. Is that a problem?"

To her credit, CC met her stare head-on. "With you being wealthy, no. But I'm not gonna lie and say imposter syndrome isn't playing a symphony in my head right now."

"Do you want to know what I'm most proud of in this office?"

CC's gaze slid to the Central Park photo on the wall. "That?"

Al smiled and held up two fingers. "Close second."

"Did you take the photo?"

"No, but it was the thing I bought with my first summer associate paycheck." She crossed to the bookcase and retrieved the faded green Dom Perignon coffin off the middle shelf. "This is third. First bottle of the good stuff Ezra and I ever bought. Found it on the cheap in a corner liquor store near the courthouse the day we were married."

She opened the box and withdrew the yellowed slip of cardstock nestled beside the empty bottle inside. "But this is number one." She handed the business card to CC.

CC flipped it over, a divot forming between her brows. "A family attorney in New York City? Was he a mentee or something?"

She shook her head. "Remember Noah from the kitchen?"

CC nodded. "Ezra's husband."

"Before that, he was Tyler's childhood best friend. He and his father lived across the hall from us, and for too long, we missed the abuse his father inflicted on him. Because Noah was gay. When we found out, I gave him that card so he could emancipate himself, we gave him a stack of bills, and Ezra got him out of town. Thirteen years later, Noah gave that card back to me the day he married Ezra." She leaned against the desk beside CC and slipped the card from her hand. "Noah came home to us. All of this"—she gestured at the wet bar, at the big TV, at the house—"it's superficial. What matters most are people, and the love you share, and the *home* you create." She splayed a hand over her heart, over the card. "Here."

CC remained silent a few long moments, curling her fingers around the edge of the table, staring out at the pool. Al was getting used to these pauses with her. CC took the time to arrange her thoughts and consider her words, something Al could appreciate. She'd been better at it earlier in her career; she cared less about it these days.

"Do you still love him? Ezra?" CC asked, and Al

appreciated the frankness too, that CC had considered and asked the question so many tiptoed around.

"I will always love and need Ezra. This is *our* family. But our romantic and sexual needs diverged in recent years."

"I'm glad you still have that. The love and friendship."

"I'm sorry someone broke yours."

The seeming non sequitur caused CC to whip her head to the side, bringing them nose to nose. "My what?"

"Trust." CC's brown eyes widened, not so non sequitur any longer. Al's suspicion had been right. Was the rest? "Makes being an exhibitionist sub hard, I imagine."

Her eyes widened further, then fluttered closed. A deep breath later, the tension in CC's frame eased on a chuckle. She hung her head. "I haven't even broached the scene since I moved here."

"Six years?"

CC angled her face, smiling. "Now you sound like the honking geese. And no, I've not gone six years without sex."

"Just not with the sex you need."

She shifted her gaze back toward the house. "Our family is close. Not big like yours, but close and accepting. I'm a lesbian, Colby is pan and poly; our parents never blinked, no matter who or how many partners we brought home. So I trusted other people. Too easily, it turned out."

"That trust burned you?"

"I thought there was room for me somewhere there wasn't, professionally and personally."

"Ah." So on top of how overwhelmed any person

would feel being thrown into one of Al's family gatherings, the situation had set off a particular trigger for CC. "And all this looks awfully crowded."

Her smile was sheepish, and a lovely blush creeped up her neck. "You invited me here. I should be grateful."

Al scooted closer and laid a hand over CC's on the table. "It's just you and me here." A crash rang out from the house on the other side of the pool. "And three giant chefs in my kitchen, but ignore that."

CC laughed, the last of her tension evaporating, and Al swooped into the opening, pushing off the table and moving to stand between CC's legs. She reached out her hand and brushed back the long red strands that had tempted her the past two weeks. CC had blown her curls out straight tonight, the silk and shine like a Broadway theater curtain. "I'm not going to argue your imposter syndrome," Al said. "Lord knows I've had my bouts with it. Any woman in our profession has. Which is why we have to lift each other up. Why it hurts all the more when women are the people who break our trust and break us down." She curled a finger under CC's chin and lifted it, waiting for CC's gaze to meet hers. "I won't break yours, CC. I won't break you."

"I'm starting to believe that," CC said, so soft, so inviting; it was all Al could do to lower her hand and step back. To not steal the kiss she so badly wanted. She couldn't stifle the groan of frustration that escaped, though.

CC smiled, wicked and tempting, and Al shook a finger at her. "Put that smirk away. We're not going there until we close this deal, like we agreed. That's part of building the trust between us. What you need to believe."

"What if I get there sooner?"

"Stop being a lawyer for two seconds."

"A horny lawyer," CC said.

Al stepped back between her legs and clasped her thighs, squeezing gently. "Tony's right, you're trouble too." She leaned forward, a brush of lips to tide them both over. "I want to give you what you need, CC. We're not there yet, but I promise when we do get there, it'll be worth it."

Chapter Thirteen

CC stood outside the conference room door, listening as Al explained tomorrow's zoning hearing to Brynn. CC and Brynn wouldn't be attending. Dotson was the party petitioning for an expanded license. Jen and Etienne didn't need to be at the hearing, so neither did CC or Brynn, who were expected at the firm holiday party tomorrow night anyway.

Al had lucked out of that one. Not that the zoning hearing would be much more pleasant, the way she was explaining it to Brynn. She patiently answered Brynn's follow-up questions, sharing her knowledge and experience with the junior associate. Too rare these days.

When it sounded like they were wrapping up, Brynn with a "Thanks for the walk-through," CC pushed off the wall and into the conference room.

Al glanced in her direction. "You get your other transaction signed?"

Jen and Etienne weren't the only ones trying to finish

year-end deals. CC had been negotiating a franchise agreement for another client that had taken an unexpected turn last week, leaving Brynn and Al to keep the Tchin Tchin deal moving forward while she juggled matters. "Finally." She lowered into the chair on the other side of Brynn. "So I can finally turn my full attention to this one. Where are we on the checklist?" she asked Brynn.

Brynn drew her laptop closer and opened the deal management app they were using to organize the transaction.

"Technology, man," Al muttered from her other side.

CC chuckled. "A long way from the paper checklists and accordion files."

"Happy to have missed that era," Brynn mumbled.

CC playfully shoved her shoulder. "Just for that, I'm going to pull out the accordion for the recordable docs on this deal."

"Fair," Brynn conceded with a nod. CC really had gotten lucky in the associate lottery. Granted, she'd had a string of entitled frat boys to endure before Brynn had walked through MRM's doors, but karma had rewarded her in the end. "APA is pending exhibits," Brynn said. "Exhibits are pending final diligence items."

She glanced past Brynn to Al, a brow raised.

"Environmental report is due today," Al said. "I'll read through it, then make any changes we need for the reps and warranties exhibit. In the meantime, I uploaded revisions on the ancillary docs for your review."

"Funding?" CC asked as Brynn scrolled to that part of the checklist.

"I'm expecting loan documents any day now."

"Cutting it a little close."

"We're not the only year-end deal."

"I know, I know."

"They're gonna want copies of all the ancillaries," Al said. "So the sooner we button those up, the better."

"I'm on it," CC said. "And let us know whatever else you need for the opinion letter." Legal opinions—or fancy cover-your-ass letters—were always one of the last and trickiest items negotiated in a financing transaction, and they required everything else to be done before they could be issued.

"In that case," CC said, rotating her chair toward Brynn, "I think we're done for the night."

"Excellent." Brynn clicked a few boxes on her electronic checklist, sent an email that vibrated on arrival in CC's inbox, then snapped her laptop shut. "See you tomorrow," she said to CC as she stood, then to Al as she gathered her things, "Good luck at the hearing."

She was barely out the door when Al tossed her glasses onto the table and kicked her bare feet up into the vacated chair.

"Make yourself at home," CC said sarcastically, even as she did exactly the same, her feet toward the back of the chair, only a couple inches apart.

"Feels like it the past few weeks." She looked around the conference room, her gaze landing back on CC. "Not that the view's been tough to look at."

CC kicked a foot against Al's in the chair. "Behave." Truthfully, it was the last thing CC wanted Al to do at this point. In the ten days since First Night dinner at Al's place, Al had kept her distance while keeping CC on the edge with her teasing. Close proximity, soft, tactile touches, little snippets of their lives and likes shared over coffee and lunch, but nothing further. She was giving them space for trust to grow. And it had, though perhaps the thing that had won Al the most trust was the way she carefully handled the transaction, Brynn, and the MRM firm staff.

CC leaned the rest of the way back in the chair. "You're a good teacher."

"I actually convinced Ezra to be a teacher for six months before he moved to Sonoma." She drew her phone out of her pocket, glanced at the screen, then laid it facedown on the table next to her discarded glasses. "I think maybe both of us would have gone into academia if we hadn't needed to make a living ASAP. We had Ty when I was twenty and Ezra was twenty-three. It took Ezra having heart issues in his midfifties for us both to realize we needed to slow down."

CC started upright in her chair. The man she'd met at Al's place had seemed in perfect health. "Is he okay?"

"Better than," Al said with a smile. "The sabbatical was good for him."

"That whole new husband thing."

"Yeah, *that*," Al said with an even bigger grin. "Also gave me the courage to accept the secondment here. I had been climbing for so long that dedicating this much time to one client was impossible. It's a nice change to dig in with one sole client as my focus."

"To build that trust."

"Exactly." Al gestured out the window on the other side of the table, the Superdome lit black and gold for game night. "And not a bad place to do it, especially with Greg, Tony, and Amos here. But I do miss the teaching aspect of being in a firm."

"Well, thank you for working with Brynn while you're here." Today hadn't been the only day CC had eavesdropped on lessons with Al. "You don't have to as opposing counsel, but it's appreciated. And I think she likes the nasal lilt of home."

"Hey now." A slightly harder kick against her foot, and CC parried back. Neither moved to untangle their feet as Al's gaze drifted back out the window. "I can't imagine. I stayed in New York for school."

"I didn't go far either. Stanford Law after graduating from Berkeley, and with my girlfriend too." Al's gaze snapped back to hers, and CC immediately diverted hers the direction Al's had been, out the window, hiding the truth in her eyes, if not her words. "On second thought, maybe a fresh start is good."

She was surprised Al didn't immediately step into the opening. Instead, she withdrew her feet, stood, and ambled over to the drink cart in the far corner. "This is the great thing about firms here. You always have booze."

It took her less than two minutes for Al to return with tumblers for each of them. CC figured she knew the drink by color and smell, but one sip and there was a familiar twist. "You put the extra spoonful of cherry juice in your Manhattans like Tony does."

"Believe it or not, we learned it from the same bartender in Manhattan." She leaned close and lowered her voice. "Tony doesn't know it, but that bartender is one of the kinkiest fuckers in New York City."

Laughter bubbled out of CC, and with it, some of her caution. "Have you gotten into the scene here?" she asked Al. They'd talked around it before, but never directly.

"I went to several parties in the spring, but haven't had —or rather, made time since work picked back up. Ezra keeps giving me lists of folks to contact." She smiled around a sip of her drink. "I'll scene with his vineyard manager when I'm in town there, he's an old friend of ours, but it's also hard to start over at fifty-six in a new town."

CC took a long sip of her Manhattan, remembering the first time she'd had her favorite cocktail. It was her twentieth birthday; her first sex party too. "Quinn, that was my girlfriend," she said, sharing some of the memory with Al, "we met in the prelaw fraternity at Berkeley. She was from San Francisco and knew the scene. I'd always known I liked women, and I'd always gotten a thrill out of public displays of affection. It wasn't until I met Quinn that I realized it was more than that."

"Quinn was a Domme too?" Al slid her feet back onto the chair next to CC's. Maybe that was what made answering her question easier.

"Yes, though not a particularly good one when I think about the others we met or watched at parties. But I was twenty and in love."

"And you made it all through law school together too?"

"She popped the question on graduation day." It was

hard not to smile at that memory, at the joy she could remember like it was yesterday. "I'd never been happier. Let her tie me to a St. Andrews cross that night."

"I didn't peg you for a masochist."

"I'm not. It was about the exhibition, and she minded my pain tolerance that night. Few years later, we ended up on opposite sides of a deal, and my client walked away with the better end of it." She drained the rest of her Manhattan. "Quinn let the professional bleed into the personal. There wasn't room for us both there."

"I'm sorry. Losing that trust can be devastating."

CC ran her nail along the rim of her empty glass, remembering jagged ones from her past. "It wouldn't have been as bad at the end if she hadn't let it bleed the other way too. After I called off the engagement, word got around professionally in circles that didn't understand."

"That's why you left San Francisco?"

"Colby saw me spiraling. She announced she was going to New Orleans to learn to make beignets and asked if I wanted to come with her." It really wasn't an ask so much as an I-will-make-you-biscuits-every-day-if-that's-what-I-have-to-do-to-save-you bribery. CC had seen it for what it was—Colby taking care of her, making room, creating an escape hatch—and she loved her all the more for it.

"You've done well here," Al said, bringing them back to the present. "I looked you up too. Your peers admire you, and you do good work."

"But I've kept a whole part of myself closed off."

Al removed her legs again from the chair, and CC

missed the closeness immediately. Until Al nudged the chair with CC's legs still in it away from the table, enough to slide her own chair closer. She nudged CC's hand to let go of the glass, then gently clasped it, tangling their fingers. "For good reason, CC. You open it up when you're ready. No one, including me, should push you do that before then."

"But when I'm ready . . ." She lifted her gaze, not sure what she'd find in Al's, then gasping—Al's dark eyes had gone molten, reflecting every bit of growing desire CC felt for her.

"I won't tie you to a cross. I'm not a sadist. Pain to that degree doesn't do it for me. But I will be happy to show others how well you take orders. Whether it's one person or a full room, they will want to be you, because you are smart, beautiful, powerful, and you deserve to be worshipped. I will show them that you are not the imposter. Would you like that, CC?"

If the experience on the airplane, if the kiss in the office at Dram, were any indication, sex with Al—the sex she needed, that Al was promising—would be amazing. "Very much."

Chapter Fourteen

Al was halfway up the never-ending escalators when her phone, already in her hand, vibrated. She glanced at the name on-screen and smiled. Exactly the person she wanted to talk to. She lifted the phone to her ear. "You hanging in there, Red?"

CC heaved a giant sigh. "Barely." She barely got the word out when Wham!'s "Last Christmas" began blasting in the background. An impossibly heavier sigh echoed over the line. "Party's still going."

As if Al couldn't hear that from the floor above. "Is there someplace quiet you can escape to?" Translation: *Tell me exactly where to find you.*

"Yeah, the terrace furthest away from the DJ."

"Which view?" On the cab ride over, Al had distracted herself from the Drakkar Noir–soaked cab driver by looking this place up. On the top floor of a four-story building right on the water, it had amazing views from all angles—the river and bridge, the skyline, the Quarter. It was a perfect spot for MRM's holiday party.

"Dauphin," CC said.

"Grab a sweater. It's finally cold out." From when Al had entered the government building for the zoning hearing that afternoon to when she had finally escaped an hour ago, the temperature had dropped a good twenty degrees, finally making it feel like winter. Not NYC winter, but still on the colder end of what she'd experienced in New Orleans so far.

"I will take the cold over Whamageddon. Maybe no one else will be out there." A prospect Al could get behind too. "Give me a minute to run the gauntlet."

Al went on mute herself, finally reaching the top floor. The double doors in front of her were decorated with garlands and red ribbons, a sign next to them confirming the location of the MRM holiday party. She peeked inside. The period of the night where the lawyers who'd had too much to drink were dancing poorly was firmly in effect. Uninhibited attorneys aside, the setting was elegant from what she could see in the dim lighting. Garland wrapped candles on each white-clothed table; red, green, and gold balloons nestled in the coffered ceiling; a buffet table piled high with desserts in front of the half-moon windows that overlooked the river.

A bar immediately to her left with no line.

She cinched her coat tightly around her, severely undressed as she was among all the sparkly holiday finery, and quickly sneaked inside. She asked the bartender if there was a shortcut to the Dauphin terrace and slipped him a Benjamin for the half-full Sazerac bottle on his back-bar. The shortcut put her on the green couch beneath the tinseled NOLA sign just in time to witness CC come through the terrace doors.

And fuck, what a sight she was.

She'd eschewed green and red for black, a figure-hugging, long-sleeved, off-the-shoulders leotard with a sheer black organza skirt that fell from a silk strip of fabric at her waist. A slit in the skirt swished open with each step she took, revealing a teasing glimpse of long legs and the sexiest pair of red snakeskin fuck-me heels Al had ever seen.

"Eyes up here," CC said, and when Al lifted her gaze, she met CC's amused grin. If the rocking body hadn't been torture enough, her smoky eyes and blush lips, her hair was straightened and teased to max volume, were the cappers that pushed Al over the edge. She uncapped the Sazerac and took a healthy swig straight from the bottle. "I thought I said grab a coat."

"I'm hot."

"No shit." She raked her gaze over the entire gorgeous woman again. "I cannot be the only person giving you looks tonight."

CC continued to glide toward her. "You're not."

"You look amazing."

"I know." She stopped in front of her, plucked the bottle from her hand, and turned it up, taking an even healthier swig.

"That's not helping, Red."

"Neither is you sitting there all casual-like." She

handed back the bottle. "Hiding God only knows what under that trench."

"A boring-ass suit."

"You haven't worn a boring-ass suit since the day you walked into Tchin Tchin." She stepped closer and reached out a hand, a finger slipping beneath the gold scarf Al had paired with her suit today. "And these *ties* have been torturing me every day since." She twirled it around her finger, and if Al hadn't already been wet between her legs, she was now. "If there weren't a room full of my work colleagues behind us . . ."

Al hooked her left leg around the back of CC's right one, low enough hopefully not to be noticed, but tight enough to keep her close. "You'd do what, Red? Tell me."

"I'd straddle your lap so you could feel how hot I was for you." The little tug she gave the tie nearly made Al come on the spot.

She tipped the bottle up and took another swig to calm herself. "And if we didn't have a deal to close first."

CC's pout was epic. "You're mean." She untangled their feet and sank onto the couch next to Al. "Don't get me wrong, I'm happy and turned the fuck on to see you, but what are you doing here? Didn't you have dinner with the Dotsons after the hearing?"

"They were a no-show."

CC's casual demeanor jumped off the building. She sat up straight, whirling in Al's direction. "They what?"

"I handled it. We got the variance."

"That's not an answer." Her dark brows were pinched, a deep V between them. "I thought it was important to them." Her voice was as circumspect as her expression. She had every right to be. Al would be too if she were on CC's side of the deal. But there was a more mundane explanation in this case.

"It is, but Mother Nature doesn't give a flying fuck about our deal. Snow in DC grounded everything, including Bo's plane on the runway at Dulles."

Her features eased a measure. "Will that get here in time to sign Friday?"

"That's the plan, as far as I know." Loan docs had dropped today, as had the environmental report, and to spare everyone the headache of signing the week between Christmas and New Year's, they were signing on Friday, ahead of the holiday week. "But CC, we don't have to table close this if the weather continues to be a bitch."

She relaxed back against the sofa. "I know. It's just safer than shuttling the couple of wet ink docs we need. I had a colleague once whose closing docs were on a carrier plane that ran off the runway."

"Oof, I'm sorry for them." Al matched her posture, legs crossed her direction, their elbows brushing against the back of the couch. "And I get that you also want to make this special for Jen and Etienne."

"E-signatures are so impersonal. Fine for the random office building or data center, but this is their dream they're selling. They deserve more than a digital confirmation for what they built."

Al wedged the bottle of rye between her hip and the back of the couch, then reached out a hand to brush back a flyaway strand of red. "You're amazing, you know that?"

"I do." She glanced up through her long, burnished lashes. "But the reminders don't hurt."

Al twirled the strand around her finger. "I really want to take you to bed tonight." Not the first time, not by a long shot, but tonight the need was supercharged. Between the stars overhead, the warmth of the whiskey, and CC looking like the tastiest snack she'd ever seen—not to mention CC putting her heart out there like the decent human she was—her mood was like Colby's doughnuts: sugary, tart, and full of the promise of goodness.

"Doesn't sound like a bad idea." CC shifted closer, the slit in her skirt opening, the organza falling behind her knee and giving Al more fantasies than she ever needed of those thighs stretched across her lap.

Fantasies *only*, for now, but that didn't mean Al couldn't share some of those wicked thoughts with CC. "Soon," she said as she hitched her own crossed knees higher, blocking anyone from seeing her hand breach the space between them and land on CC's lower thigh. "For now I'm gonna tell you what you're gonna go home and do tonight."

CC's eyes cut to the ballroom doors she'd exited minutes ago.

"You liked it earlier," Al said. "The thought of straddling my lap with a room full of people watching." CC opened her mouth to voice the caveat, but Al beat her to it. "*If* they weren't your colleagues."

"But they are, and I can't . . ."

"I know."

Al moved to withdraw her hand, but CC clasped her

wrist, keeping Al's palm pressed to her thigh, then inched it higher so Al's fingertips were brushing just inside the juncture of her thighs, right above her clit. "I can't go any further than this, not here."

Al could feel the damp material, could feel the trembles that rippled through CC, shivers that had nothing to do with the cool breeze whipping around them. "Can I continue?" she said, voice lowered, her middle finger drawing the lightest of circles, teasing CC through layers of material. She couldn't reach her clit in this position, but stroking near it was having the intended effect, judging by the breathiness of CC's reply.

"Tell me, what am I gonna do when I get home?" CC retrieved the whiskey bottle with her hand not resting on Al's wrist and tipped it back for a sip, keeping up the ruse of two colleagues sharing a drink.

"You got a dildo?" Al asked.

"I do."

"A pillow to hold it?"

"I do."

"I knew you were naughty." Al grinned as the scene came the rest of the way together in her head, the mental picture causing her own clit to throb. "If we were somewhere I could slide my hand down and palm your cunt, would I find snaps on your leotard?"

She nodded.

"And if I unsnapped the gusset?"

"Nothing."

Al whistled low and shifted, the pressure between her own legs riding her hard. "Fuck, Red."

CC's fingers around her wrist tightened, nails digging near her pulse point. "Tell me how."

Al reined herself back in and increased the speed and pressure of her strokes. "You're gonna go home, you're gonna leave all this on, including those heels, and you're gonna set the pillow and dildo up on your bed facing the window. Lights off, blinds open."

CC's eyes fluttered closed, her chest heaving, the curves of her breasts fighting the neckline of the leotard. "Okay," she panted. "Now what?"

Al kept going, painting the erotic picture for her. "You're gonna climb on the bed, unsnap the leotard, then sink down on that dildo."

CC groaned and parted her legs enough for Al to rub lower, closer to her clit. "Fuck yeah."

"You're going to ride it like you're putting on a show for me. Like it's me under you, my strap-on you're grinding down on, my fingers stroking your clit." She increased the pressure again and, with her other hand dangling from the back of the couch, flirted with the side of CC's breast. "And I want you to pull these amazing tits out of your bra, over this tempting fucking neckline, and hold them in your hands, squeeze and pinch them until you're right on the edge."

Sweat dappled CC's forehead, her breaths coming fast and short. "And then?"

"And then you're gonna fall forward and put your hands in the mattress above my head, your tits in my face. And I'm going to suck so hard you scream loud enough for the neighbors to hear when you *come*."

Her body stiffened, jerked, and then heat and wetness intensified against Al's fingertips. "Fuck me."

"I intend to, Red." She leaned closer, as if whispering something to anyone watching, and chanced a lick of the sweat that dappled CC's hairline. CC gave another jerk, and Al grinned. "You're so responsive, so good for me."

A devastating whimper.

"We close this deal, and I'm gonna fuck you good, CC. I'll give you everything you need, just the way you like it."

CC's eyes fluttered open, the warm brown molten. "Promise?"

"Promise."

Chapter Fifteen

CC checked each of the folders in the accordion file sorters on the conference table. Everything was in order. Only two empty slots left.

"I've got 'em." Brynn entered the room, two folders in hand. "Final docs for wet sigs tomorrow." She dropped them into their slots. "When you said you were going to make me do the wet docs like this, I didn't actually believe you."

CC chuckled. "Al and I agreed." Along with several other less professional agreements CC was hoping to make reality this weekend. Sure, closing technically wasn't until next week, but once the documents were signed and at the title company, all that was left was for money to flow and documents to record. This torture was almost over, unbelievably ahead of schedule for a change.

"It's important for Jen and Etienne," CC explained. "And yes, ninety percent of closings are digital now, but"—she tapped the accordion of documents on the left—"deeds and recordables still require wet ink in most jurisdictions." Then tapped the accordion on the right. "And Dotson's lender is insisting on at least one set of wet signed documents too. A pain, yes, but you've done great work getting this all set up."

"There is something cathartic about seeing it ready to go like this."

"For my first big solo closing, I had two rows of accordions and folders stretched down a table twice this long."

"See, now, that's not catharsis, that's just madness."

They were both still laughing when Deena leaned her head into the conference room. "I'm sending a call through to you."

"Who is it?" CC asked.

"Jen. Doesn't sound good."

The worry ripples from early in the deal resurfaced, tossing CC's mostly coffee stomach with them. The same anxiety had briefly reared its head on Tuesday night when Al had told her about the Dotsons being no-shows at the hearing, but there'd been a perfectly good explanation for that. Had there been more to it? Was that why Jen was calling? Or was there a different hiccup? There honestly hadn't been enough of them yet for this to feel real.

The call rang through to the conference table phone, and Brynn pressed the Speaker button to answer. "Hey Jen, this is Brynn. I've got CC with me. We're just getting ready for tom—"

"There's a fucking surveyor at Tchin Tchin," she said, voice practically a growl.

"We already have a survey," CC said.

"They fucking did it, CC. I knew it. I knew they were going to. Bo had to have known yesterday when I called to confirm dinner tomorrow and he still said we were a go. That fucking liar."

"Jen, calm down a second and keep your voice down." She didn't know how close said surveyor was, but CC guessed close from the whispered volume of Jen's voice initially. "Tell me what's going on."

She took a deep breath, and started over, volume lowered again. "There's a surveyor here who was hired by the Mosley Group."

"The same Mosleys that own the office building across the street?"

"The very same," Jen said. "According to the surveyor, he just needs to mark the corners of the lot since the structure will be torn down for a parking deck."

CC's stomach hit the floor, a tidal wave threatening to take her knees out next. She leaned a hip against the table. "They can't. It's historical."

"It's not technically on the register," Brynn said. Something they'd been grateful for—less paperwork and approvals—up until this point.

"Call," she told Brynn. "Find out if we can make it happen."

"It's the Thursday before a holiday weekend," Jen said.

"We have to try."

Brynn scurried out the door while CC leaned over the phone, both hands on the table. "Sit tight, Jen, and let's see what we can find out."

"I'm not selling only for this place to be bulldozed."

"I wouldn't let you." Technically, she couldn't stop them, but she could strongly advise against it. She knew Jen and Etienne well enough to know they would regret selling out to see their dream handled so carelessly.

Including by Al.

Disappointment settled heavy in CC's gut, taking up residency with the swirling coffee. She was disappointed for Jen and Etienne and for herself. But she couldn't let the latter show; her client had to be her top priority right now. "You haven't signed anything yet, no funds are in motion, there's no deal."

"I thought you said we could trust them."

"I thought we could too."

Chapter Sixteen

One look at CC barreling through Dram's door, and Al figured the Vieux Carré she'd ordered as a peace offering was more likely to end up in her face. She drew the drink closer instead and took a fortifying gulp. At least it was still midafternoon, before Dram opened to customers. Only the staff would bear witness to their argument; without other patrons crowding the space, CC reached her side in mere seconds.

Eyes hard and color high on her cheeks, she shoved the barstool beside Al out of the way and crowded close. "Did you know?" she demanded, the normal huskiness of her voice morphing into a rumbling anger.

"CC—"

"You know that property means something to Jen and Etienne—and to me—and you're just going to let Dotson sell it off for a parking garage?"

"You know as well as I do that I don't let my clients do anything. They let me work for them."

CC slammed her palm on the bar. "That's bullshit! You're practically in-house counsel."

"But I'm not."

A third voice entered the fray. "Whoa," Colby said, sliding in next to her sister. "What's going on here?"

"Professional disagreement," Al replied quickly. She was sure CC could give a more colorful explanation that would forever damn her in Colby's eyes, and Colby's opinion mattered. If Al ever wanted a shot with CC, she'd need Colby's approval.

"Well, Amos is in the kitchen with Greg and Tony"—Colby lowered her voice—"and now he wants to know what *bullshit* means."

"Fuck," CC muttered as she dragged a hand down her weary face.

"Let's not add that one too." Colby handed Al Tony's key ring. "Take it to the office and give me a few minutes to get the mixer going before the cursing starts again."

She marched back to the kitchen, and Al swiveled on her stool, an arm out for CC to lead the way. It was a tense couple seconds—would CC hear her out or storm away?—but eventually she stepped back and turned toward the office.

Al downed the rest of the cocktail, then followed in CC's wake, admiring the view of the gorgeous, pissed-off woman she'd hoped to finally get in her bed this weekend. Her red curls swayed like flames against the midnight blue of her sweater, her strides were long and determined, and today's charcoal pencil skirt perfectly framed her ass and thighs.

She unlocked the office door, then cut a sharp glance over her shoulder. "Stop staring at my as—bottom."

Al shrugged on her way into the office. "It's a fine tush."

"You're not going to flirt your way out of this."

She waited for CC to close the door, then raised both hands, palms out. "I didn't know about Rob's plan to sell the real estate until this afternoon."

CC leaned back against the closed door. "Rob's plan?"

Al circled one of the visitor chairs and nudged it with her toe to angle it in CC's direction before sinking into it. It was a negotiation tactic Ezra had taught her—if you were negotiating from the position of power, make yourself physically smaller or lower to get the other party onto your side. Less threatening was better. In this case, she'd gladly give all the power back to CC if it were in her hands to do so. "He's been working with Kip, Dotson's in-house counsel and his old frat buddy, behind my and Bo's backs. And it might interest you to know Kip and Rob are also in the same fraternity as your boss and with one of the higher-ups at Mosley."

One of CC's brows raced north. "Ted?" Al nodded, and CC's other brow raced to match. "Ted told them?"

"Someone put a bug in their ear. I only found out about it this afternoon when the title agent called me about issues on the second deed from Dotson to Mosley."

"And then what happened?"

"I called Bo immediately."

"Doesn't Bo have the final say?"

"He wants the whiskey."

"At what cost?"

Al leaned toward Tony and Greg's ever-cluttered desk for a pen and paper. She jotted down the figure, tore off the corner of paper, then held the slip out to CC. "I'm authorized to negotiate up to that amount."

CC's eyes flared wide—Bo was offering almost double the original offer—then narrowed as she shifted her gaze back to Al. "Is this for real?"

"I'm not going to"—she lowered her voice—"bullshit you. I do understand what this deal means to you and to Jen and Etienne. That's the ceiling of what Bo will pay. You have to take it to your client."

CC stared at the slip of paper again. "You're asking them to make an impossible decision."

"I'm not the one asking."

CC's gaze shot back to her, harder even than when she'd first walked through Dram's door. "Fuck you."

"CC—"

She pushed off the door and stood directly in front of Al, glaring down at her. "I trusted you. With this deal, with my friends, with my associate, with my hope. I wanted—" She cut off her words and spun in the other direction, lunging for the door.

Al shot out of her chair. "If I'd known—"

Then rocked back on her heels when CC rounded on her. "You would've done what? Just offered sooner? Your client doesn't intend to stick around. They're just going to take what they want and leave."

Like you. CC didn't have to speak the words for Al to hear them.

And Al didn't have to be a genius to know CC needed time and space to process. This wasn't just any client, it wasn't just any deal, and it wasn't just a professional relationship between them anymore. In truth, it never had been.

It hurt like hell to step back, but there would be no moving forward if Al kept pushing. And she wanted to move forward—with CC. She wanted to find out if the spark that had grown brighter the past month could lead to the raging inferno they'd only glimpsed in a few stolen moments.

She gave CC space and rested back against the front of the desk. "You have to know, CC, this is not how I wanted things to go."

Know, maybe; *believe* was a harder sell, judging by the anger that morphed into pain in CC's eyes and voice. "I trusted you. And now I may lose two of my best friends because of that mistake."

Al wanted to cross the office and wrap CC in her arms. Wanted to assure her that no one would blame her and that she was still one of the best and brightest attorneys she'd ever worked with. Wanted to tell her that while the Dotsons might take what they want and leave, she wouldn't. Instead, she curled her fingers around the desk's edge and forced herself to stay still. To give CC the time and space she needed. "I'm sorry, CC. Truly."

CC's "Me too" was a fraction of her earlier outburst . . . and exponentially more devastating.

Chapter Seventeen
____

Thank fuck for eggnog, Christmas trees, and first cousins once removed. CC's parents were so distracted by Colby's heavy-handed pours and their cousins' kids that CC was able to use the giant tree as cover and sneak out of the white elephant exchange unnoticed. She swung through the kitchen, refreshed her mug of mulled wine, then ventured outside.

Her childhood home was a modest midseventies rancher that, like most California homes, no longer had a modest price tag. Her parents had used the mountain of home equity to periodically update and renovate, most recently the large backyard patio that overlooked the golf course between their neighborhood and the luxury ocean-front resort.

The new trellis over the patio table was draped with fragrant garland and twinkling white lights, and the firepit that bisected the outdoor space still burned from earlier when the adults had gathered outside for drinks.

It was cooler now, but not so cold that CC's sweater, plus the wine and fire, weren't enough to keep her toasty.

If only her insides were as warm. After burning red-hot with Al the night of the firm holiday party, a chill had settled over her since Thursday. It had started in her belly when she'd first heard the parking garage news, had worked its way into her chest as she'd argued with Al at Dram, then had wrapped around her heart as she'd given Jen and Etienne the fuller picture later that evening. They'd been confused, conflicted, and hurt most of all. There had been no Friday signing. The parties would touch base again on Tuesday after the holiday and decide whether to proceed.

In the days since, CC had received several texts from Al, the last vibrating mid-dinner, a **Merry Christmas Eve** message. CC had left it on read like she had the others, not yet ready to engage, not even sure what she would say. She was hurt too, and all the Christmas cheer in the world wasn't going to fix her wounded hope.

The patio door opened behind her, and the familiar squeak of Crocs was a dead giveaway. If that hadn't been enough, the dessert plate that appeared in front of her, two slices of pumpkin roll on either side of a chocolate one, would have confirmed her visitor's identity.

"I thought you only made the two Yule logs," she said to her sister.

Colby hiked up her green and gold dress and threw one leg, then the other, over the bench to sit beside her. "Pumpkin's your favorite, and you don't love chocolate like the rest of humanity." Colby held up two spoons. "But you're gonna share."

They cleaned the plate in companionable silence, the muted strains of Christmas music from inside and the distant crash of waves floating softly in the night air around them. Until Colby disturbed the calm, as was her way. "Mom and Dad may not have noticed your disappearing act, but I did."

"I needed a breather from all the cheer."

Colby bumped a shoulder against hers. "I'm sorry this isn't the holiday celebration you wanted."

"Deals die all the time." She dragged her spoon through Colby's standout cranberry coulis. "And this one still may not."

"I wasn't only talking about the deal."

She licked her spoon clean, then traded it for her mug of wine. "You seem more invested in things working between me and Al than you've been with anyone else I've dated. And we're not even technically dating. Why?"

Colby side-eyed her. "You basically were, and even if you technically weren't, you wanted to."

CC bumped her shoulder back. "Answer the question."

"Because she's your match. And—" She bit her lip in an uncharacteristic display of hesitation.

Ripples of worry that CC was becoming all too familiar with lately creeped up her spine. She set aside her mug. "And?"

"And I don't want you to be alone."

The worry receded. Colby was just looking out for her.

See: pumpkin roll. CC wrapped an arm around her sister's shoulders. "I'm not alone. I have you."

"But I won't be with you much longer."

CC froze, a tsunami appearing out of nowhere and bowling her under the waves. She sank, all that ice drifting around her heart the past few days now freezing into an iceberg at Colby's words, taking her down. "What? What's wrong?" Every worst-case scenario screamed through her head.

"Nothing bad," Colby rushed to clarify, a hand on her forearm. She angled toward CC, their knees bumping under the table. "I, umm . . ." She flicked her gaze down to the empty plate, then back up to CC's. "I got a job offer that was too good to pass up."

Oh. *Oh!* The banter CC couldn't follow in Al's kitchen at Hanukkah suddenly made sense. "Miller or Noah?"

"Miller," Colby said, the corners of her mouth fighting a smile. "I'd be his head pastry chef, running his pastry and bread lines for his restaurant, Chess, and for the ground floor storefront they have in the building."

"Shit, Colby."

Her smile died. "I'm sorry, I know the timing sucks—"

CC threw her arm back around her sister and hugged. The last thing she wanted to do was make Colby feel guilty for jumping at an amazing, well-earned opportunity. "No, Colby, don't you dare apologize for being an awesome chef that another awesome chef recognized."

Colby heaved a giant sigh and relaxed against her side. "I wanted you and Al to work out so you'd have someone in New Orleans. I know you'll stay. You love it there, and you don't do snow."

Laughter beat out the lonely panic scratching at CC's throat. "I hated those ski weeks in Tahoe."

"She's good for you too," Colby continued, undeterred. "I've seen you smile more the past month than you have in six years."

"I need to be able to trust her, Col. We won't work without it."

Colby twisted again to face her, expression serious. "Has she given you a reason not to?"

"The deal—"

"Has *she*, CC? Al. Was she the one who actually betrayed your trust, or was she just the unfortunate messenger?"

CC reclaimed her mug and sipped at the lukewarm wine, mulling over Colby's question. While it had felt like a personal betrayal to CC, Al had looked just as betrayed that day at Dram. But she'd put aside the betrayal she'd suffered to try and fix the one against CC and her client. She'd gone to Bo, who'd done the best he could with the box others had put them all in.

"This isn't like Quinn," Colby said. "Al didn't crater the deal on purpose, and she didn't out you to anyone. At least not that I'm aware of."

CC had no indication of that either. If anything, Al had been better at respecting the boundaries CC had drawn than CC, who had wanted to blow right through them multiple times the past month. While CC's mind replayed each of those instances, Colby swung her legs out from under the table and stood.

"You're the smartest person I know, CC." She kissed the crown of her head and plucked the empty mug from her hands. "Be smart about this too."

She turned to go, but CC snagged her wrist, needing to tell her one more thing, the most important takeaway from this conversation. "I'm proud of you, Col." And the second most important. "I also expect regular care packages."

"Was already planning on it," Colby said with a wink.

Colby continued back inside, a swell of Elvis's "Blue Christmas" fittingly cresting before she shut the door behind her. Silence surrounded CC once more. The opposite of the last holiday that had been filled with light and laughter and love. A gathering that Al had gone out of her way to invite her to and make her feel welcome. She had trusted CC with her family and them with her.

CC reached for a bit of the trust from where it had been misplaced the past few days. She flipped the phone over and fired off a return text. **Merry Christmas to you too.**

Chapter Eighteen

"Was Santa good to you?"

Molly and Michael excitedly babbled over each other, telling Al all about the presents they'd unwrapped that morning and showing off whichever ones they could lay their hands on. Sloan had set up Ezra's laptop on an ottoman in front of Miller and Clancy's tree where the kiddos still sat on the floor surrounded by mounds of wrapping paper and new toys. Al breathed a sigh of relief when she spotted the sparkly reindeer paper she'd wrapped her gifts in. She was afraid they wouldn't ship there in time, given her abrupt change of plans.

"I wish he brought you, Nana," Molly said, further reminding Al of her unexpected absence and making her heart hurt more than a little.

"Nana had to work," Sloan said from nearby, off-camera. "We got to see her at Thanksgiving and Hanukkah already this year."

Molly's gaze darted between Al, her mom, and the

presents. "But what if Santa brings better gifts when Nana's here?"

Al chuckled at the little lawyer in training. "Oh, I see." Grinning, she leaned closer to the screen like she would if they were there together, right before she'd boop her grandbaby on the nose. "That's why you want me there."

"Yes!" Molly clapped and dissolved into giggles, along with Michael, who wanted to mimic his sister in everything.

Sloan was laughing too when she hauled her pajamaed kiddos to their feet and shooed them toward the kitchen. "Go, you rascals. See if lunch is ready yet." They ran out of the frame, and then the frame itself—the laptop —was being moved. Sloan didn't go far, just to the larger sofa in the room, the laptop placed on the coffee table in front of it. "That's not the only reason they want you here."

"I know, but her argument was compelling." They shared another laugh, and Al slumped into the corner of the built-in breakfast nook in Greg and Tony's kitchen. "Was Santa good to you too?"

"If by Santa you mean the giant I was once married to whose beard looks more and more like St. Nick's every year, yes. I have eaten my weight in hotel butter and cookie dough this weekend. And I feel zero guilt about it."

"Good!" Al said as she sipped from her steaming mug of chicory coffee. "You deserve the good food and the time off." Sloan had been just as busy with year-end work as she'd been, plus preparing for a cross-country trip with two kids. "And what did Tyler get you?"

"A bottle of Chateau Rayas and tickets to see *Six* on Broadway."

"That's my boy."

"He did good," Sloan said with a smile. "What about you? Did you get to spend Christmas with CC?"

"No, she's home with her family. We hit a bit of a rough patch, but I'm hopeful we'll work it out." She had woken to CC's reply text, an unexpected gift that had made the dreary Christmas morning outside brighter.

"You're a catch, Al."

"So is she."

Ty flopped onto the couch beside his wife. "What happened there? As of Thursday morning, you thought you'd still make it here."

"Client was hiding the ball. Secondary transaction, which may not even happen, that I've had to work on all weekend. Tell Miller and Clancy I'm sorry."

"It'll be all right. From the pictures you sent, you had a good Christmas morning there."

"I did." She patted her stomach and eyed the mound of dishes peeking out from the island farm sink. "Greg and Tony fed me well, and Amos was a madman with the presents."

"The madman," Tony said as he tiptoed into the kitchen, "is passed out on the couch from the breakfast food coma." He snagged two snifters and his Christmas bottle of Boss Hog and slid into the nook beside Al.

"Grandpa's on Holland nap duty here," Sloan said.

"Noah with him?" Al asked, missing her family but happy to have some of it here still.

"Try again," Clancy said as he wobbled on-screen with a bottle of champagne. He plopped onto the couch on Sloan's other side. "He and Miller are in the kitchen planning spring menus." He glanced at Sloan, then affected a conspiratorial whisper they all heard. "I forgot the orange juice."

"Good man." Sloan made grabby hands for the bottle, then drank straight from it.

Clancy clapped while Tyler rolled his eyes. "All manners are gone."

"Good," Tony said, then, with a waggle of his brows, raised his voice just enough for Greg in the other room to hear without waking Amos. "We'll drink this Pappy straight from the bottle too, then."

Al clamped a hand over her mouth, stifling her laugh, but gave up holding it in when Greg appeared in the doorway, murder in his dark eyes. He glanced at the bottle of Boss Hog, then between the two of them. "I should fucking disown you both."

"Nah, baby, you love us." Tony grinned and turned his face up for a kiss. "Get yourself a glass, Mr. New Orleans."

On the other end of the line, Tyler was handing out champagne flutes, but still no orange juice as he filled their three. Everyone lifted their glasses, toasting, "Merry Christmas."

After a sip, Greg lifted his again. "And here's hoping we have better luck next year for location two."

Tony patted his knee. "Took you four times to get it right with Dram."

Greg took a longer swallow this time. "Was hoping for three on this one."

"Did you think more about what I suggested?" Tyler leaned forward, elbows on his knees, his still mostly full flute dangling from his fingertips. "Going the speakeasy route for the time being?"

"What's this?" Al asked. A speakeasy was not something she'd heard them talk about before as an option.

"Sloan and I were at Bourbon and Branch last week," Tyler said. "And it made me think. A speakeasy could be a way to expand that wouldn't require as much space, at least not right away."

"We'd consider it," Tony said, and Greg nodded, clearly something they'd discussed since Tyler had brought it up. "Wouldn't take as much time or overhead either."

"I'd still want a food license and a small kitchen," Greg said. "For events and Sunday brunch, but we wouldn't need the kind of space we have at Dram. Simple line, that's all."

"It would do well there," Ty said. "There are plenty of places in New Orleans that are just bars, and we'd be offering something more than that. Upscale and inclusive."

"Another queer-friendly place will not go amiss," Sloan said, holding her glass up for a clink against Clancy's.

A clink that rattled a thought loose in Al's mind.

A possibility.

Hope.

She stood and scooted out of the booth.

"Mama Al," Greg said. "Where you going?"

She started opening drawers in the kitchen island,

searching. "Pen and paper?" she asked when she didn't find it in the first few, not as familiar with their kitchen as her own or the winery's.

"Drawer beside the stove," Greg said.

She crossed to the stove at the far end of the kitchen and found Greg's current recipe pad, right where he said it would be. She ripped a blank piece of paper from the back and scribbled down Tchin Tchin's address and Jen and Etienne's phone number. She returned to the booth and pushed the piece of paper across the table to her kids.

"What is this?" Greg asked as Tony picked up the future Al desperately wanted them—and her—to have.

"Your speakeasy."

Chapter Nineteen

Flying back to New Orleans from California on Christmas Day was a trick CC and Colby had learned after their first disastrous holiday travel season. That first year, they'd both been so tight on time, and Hanukkah had lined up just so, that they'd flown out Christmas Eve—a disaster—and back on Boxing Day—an even bigger disaster. Lesson learned. Flying back on Christmas Day also meant CC sometimes got an extra day off, depending on the firm holiday calendar. This year, though, she found herself at a bit of loss with the extra time. She'd expected to be working through it, gathering the final pieces of the Tchin Tchin deal to send to the title company. Instead, she was waiting on a call from Jenn and Etienne on whether they were moving forward at all.

She checked her phone one last time, then, seeing no emails or texts from them, she shoved the device in her jeans pocket, threw a sweatshirt over her tee, and made her way to the kitchen. She'd just started a pot of coffee when a knock sounded against the front door.

"No blender this morning," she hollered, assuming it was her sister. She pulled two mugs down from the cabinet, then went to open the door, surprised Colby hadn't let herself in. "I prom—"

"I can help with the no blender." Al, in a paisley patterned maxi skirt and teal sweater, stood on her front porch, holding a familiar white and green bag. "Beignets. Won't be as good as Colby's, but they'll do in a pinch."

CC couldn't help but laugh. No one had ever said *those* beignets would merely 'do in a pinch.' Credit to her sister, who yes, CC thought made better beignets too, but doughnuts, while tasty, were beside the point. "What are you doing here?" she asked Al.

"A peace offering." She held up the bag again and, at CC's cocked brow, added, "This is not all I have to offer. You'll want to hear this, CC, and it smells like you've already got the coffee going."

Yes, CC had sent Al a text on Christmas Eve, but they hadn't spoken or texted since. What exactly did she have to offer? Would it move them forward, professionally and personally, or set them back? She recalled her Christmas Eve chat with Colby, the question her sister asked. The one that had been rattling around in CC's head the past two days. Would whatever offer Al came bearing help solidify the answer, one way or the other?

She opened the door the rest of the way for Al to enter. Once inside, her eyes grew wide. "This is beautiful, CC."

"It's not the mansion you rent."

"That I *rent*. I wouldn't live there. It's too big." She cut CC a glance, then went back to surveying the surroundings. CC figured that Al, like herself, couldn't help her interest in real estate and renovations. Was maybe even more interested than even the average real estate professional given her family's ventures. She walked ahead of CC, through the living room and past the kitchen, where she dropped the bag of beignets on the granite island. She paused in the short hallway that led to the bedroom suite and glanced back, asking permission. CC nodded, and Al continued ahead. "Colby's is a mirror?"

"In dimensions," CC said. "We made individual adjustments inside our own units. Her kitchen is bigger, my bathroom is bigger."

Al stuck her head in *the CC sanctuary*, as Colby called it, and whistled low. "You don't say."

"Typical shotgun double."

"I don't think this is typical." Al ran a hand over the reclaimed wood that covered the wall behind her bed's headboard. "Are these the old floors?"

CC nodded again. "Gloria saved them for us."

"Greg's general contractor?"

"Yep, she's a miracle worker," CC said of the woman who had transformed their fixer-upper into an oasis fit for two sisters who loved to be close but also needed their own space. But for how much longer? What would CC do with the space once she left? The thought of renting it to someone else made her stomach queasy. CC shook it off, focusing on the here and now instead, on the woman in her home. She led Al back to the kitchen. "Col and I rented for a year," she said as she fetched mugs out of the cabinet and filled them with coffee. "We bought this place after Greg introduced us to Gloria. She just got it, how we wanted to transform the space yet keep the character."

"Gloria's amazing. She'll do a great job on the speakeasy."

Startled, CC bobbled the mug as she handed it to Al, splashing hot liquid on both of them. "Shit, I'm sorry."

"It's fine, CC." Al set her mug on the island and took the paper towel CC offered. "Probably shouldn't have just sprung that on you."

"It's my fault. I didn't sleep all that well." She wiped the coffee off her own hand. "Now, what speakeasy?"

"I'm violating half a dozen ethics rules here," Al said as she climbed onto one of the stools. "But since your boss did too, and nearly everyone will get what they want in the end, I hope when the dust settles it's only me on the road to early retirement."

CC shot out a hand, laying it on CC's forearm. "Don't, then." No matter what had or would happen between them, Al was too good an attorney and mentor to take herself out of the game.

She laid a hand over CC's. "I'm almost sixty, I've earned it." She chuckled, then withdrew her hand and lifted the mug to her lips, sipping.

And keeping CC in suspense. She leaned a hip against the island. "Any day now with the rest of your thought, please?"

Al chuckled, her dark eyes twinkling with mischief again. "You're not wrong about Tchin Tchin. We can't let that building be bulldozed." The twinkle turned into heat and zeroed in on CC. "And I can't let the best thing that's happened to me in years slip through my fingers."

CC set her mug aside, clearing her throat and ignoring the somersault in her belly. "We said we weren't going to make decisions on whatever this"—she gestured between them—"might be."

"And it's not the driving force." Al clasped her hand in midair and lightly tangled their fingers. "But I'm not going to claim I don't have a personal interest either."

CC lowered their hands to the island but didn't draw hers back, leaving their fingers entwined. "Okay, let's hear it."

"Your clients will be receiving a letter of intent this morning from Rosin Hospitality."

CC's fingers clenched around Al's. "Your family's company?"

"We'll offer to buy it all, but in the end, your clients will get the money they deserve, Bo will get his whiskey, and we'll buy the real estate, not Mosley. Greg and Tony will turn it into a speakeasy, and Ez and Noah will move the distilling equipment Greg and Tony don't keep for decor out to the winery. Archer, our winemaker, needs a new hobby."

"But the price tag . . ." Bo had nearly doubled his offer to keep the deal alive.

"Not an issue," Al said. "The price may come down a little because Rob won't be happy, but again—Bo will still get his whiskey, and Jen and Etienne will still get a premium and the peace of mind that their property will be well taken care of."

It was too generous an offer, and CC knew it was as much for her as it was for Jen, Etienne, and any of the Rosins. "Al, I can't—"

"It's your client's decision, not yours."

"You keep putting me in these binds."

Using the hand still in hers, Al drew her around the corner of the island and rotated on the stool so CC stood between her spread legs. "I'd like to put you in other binds if you think we can make this work." She clasped her other hand and held them together in both of hers. "And if you're not ready, that's okay too. I'll keep working to win your trust back."

"You weren't the one who broke it in the first place." She lifted her gaze, meeting Al's. "I get that now, and you and your family don't have to go to such lengths to prove it."

"My family sees a good business opportunity." She pulled her closer. "And I see what I hope is an opportunity to swan into my retirement with a smart, beautiful woman at my side." She brushed her lips against CC's cheek, making her shiver. "But know this, CC—I respect you too damn much, as an attorney and a woman, to ever use who you are against you, no matter what you decide."

CC angled in her face, lips at the corners of Al's mouth. She didn't need more time. She felt as safe as she ever hand in Al's hands. Safe enough to put her heart there too. "Let's close this deal."

Chapter Twenty

Al stood with her shoulder leaned against the opening to Dram's service area, watching her friends and family celebrate midday with the restaurant all to themselves. Didn't make it any less of a party. The winter snowflakes and lights had been swapped for gold and purple streamers and balloons, festive for New Year's and for the upcoming LSU bowl game. Greg, a tiger alum, had lined one end of the bar with appetizers, while Colby had piled the other end with desserts, leaving Tony in the middle to sling drinks.

Jen and Etienne stood close to the middle, chatting with Tony, Greg, and Tyler about plans for the speakeasy. Past them, near the desserts, CC, Colby, Brynn, and Sloan were celebrating as well, glasses of whiskey in hand. She missed Noah and Ezra, and Miller and Clancy, but someone had had to stay home with the kids. Archer, who was swaggering her way with two glasses of whiskey, had been at the closing today to represent the vineyard contingent.

He handed her the glass. "Thank you for all my new toys."

"You're welcome." She sipped the Tchin Tchin dark rye Jen and Etienne had graciously shared for the occasion. "Will it keep you interested?"

He shrugged a shoulder, his gaze skating past Al and out the window. She looped an arm through his, worried about her friend who a year ago had seemed so excited about the vineyard but now seemed distant in a way she'd never known Archer Scott to be. "What's going on, babe?"

He sipped his whiskey and hummed his appreciation.

"Good, isn't it?" she said.

"Hopefully what I make will be half this good."

"Is that what you're worried about?"

He shook his head. "I love the grapes, what we do, the wine we're making. I have no doubts about that. And in the summer when wine country is crawling, it's amazing."

"Less so in the drippy winter."

"Your ex-husband loves it."

"We're not talking about Ezra." She reached up and tilted his scruffy chin down, forcing his gaze. "Your whole life can't be the dirt and the barrels and fucking tourists in the summer, then hiding away in the winter. You're not a polar bear."

His grin was one of the sexiest she'd ever seen. Had been why she'd sent Ezra across the floor of a crowded party to fetch him that night long ago. "And your whole life can't be your work. Neither of us is cut out for that." His gaze cut across her shoulder again but this time landed squarely on CC. "You always were a sucker for a redhead."

She returned his earlier shrug, and his full barrel-chested laugh eased some of her worry. And drew said redhead's attention.

"Go get your girl," Archer said with a slap to her ass. She slapped his back, then followed his order for a change. She circled behind CC, traded her empty glass for a red velvet cupcake, then looped an arm through CC's, drawing her over to the window bench seat.

"Will we be seeing any more of the Dotsons?" CC asked.

"No, I don't think so. They're going to pause acquisitions for a while. Bo has the line he wants, Rob wants something different with the company." She flitted a hand in the air, as much a summary of the shouting match she'd witnessed that she cared to bother CC with. "They've got their own shit to sort out. This deal just made that more clear."

"So you'll be going too, then? Back to New York?"

"What I do is independent of Dotson Brands."

CC laid a hand on her crossed knees. "I'd wondered about that. I'm sorry if this deal cost you the secondment."

"Don't be. The secondment simply ran its course."

"But that's not exactly what happened, was it?"

She shrugged. Yes, if Dotson Jr. wanted to bring an ethics complaint against her, he would probably win, but she didn't think Dotson Sr. would let him given his own shady dealings. But the writing was on the wall for Dotson Brands too. Bo had his pet project, and Rob would be taking over the rest of the business. Al was more than happy to hand Rob to someone with more patience than her. But while she had that flexibility, hers wasn't the only job that could be affected. She and CC had talked about that earlier this week, and CC had decided it was worth the risk, but it was a risk nonetheless.

"What about you?" she asked. "Any fallout at MRM?"

"Status quo for now. Bosses are happy with the paycheck."

"It could have been more."

"It could have been none if we hadn't closed the deal."

"Touché." Al held up the last bite of her cupcake to toast against CC's glass. Their quiet laughter was drowned by Colby's and Sloan's at the bar.

"I'm going to miss her," CC said.

"Sloan?" Al wasn't surprised her daughter-in-law and CC had hit it off, both at the Hanukkah dinner and as Sloan had negotiated the deal documents for Rosin with her the past week.

"Yes," CC answered. "She's been great to work with and get to know better, but I meant Colby."

Al nearly choked on her last bite of cupcake. "What?"

"You didn't hear?" CC patted her back, then handed her the glass of whiskey. "Miller stole her away."

Al's eyes grew wide. "For the head pastry position at Chess?"

CC nodded.

"Fuck, I feel sorry for Greg and Tony, and I know you're gonna miss her like crazy, but Miller has been trying to fill that position forever. Colby will be a great fit. And at least she's still in the family. We can get deliveries."

"We?"

Al set the whiskey glass aside and angled on the bench toward CC, an arm behind her, the other on the table. "I'm not going back to New York either, CC. I have no immediate plans to leave New Orleans."

CC held her stare several long seconds, as if letting the words sink in, and when they finally did, the corner of her mouth turned up in that killer smirk that had hooked Al a month ago in an airport bar. "We closed the deal."

"We did." Al lowered the hand on the table to CC's thigh under the table, tracing her blunt nail up to the hem of her skirt. "And tonight, we celebrate with our families." She dove under the hem, hand clasping the inside of CC's thigh and making her gasp, a lovely blush racing up her neck to her cheeks. "And then you're going to meet me at my place tomorrow night, wearing that dress and those fuck-me heels from the Christmas party, and we'll have our own celebration." She cupped her over what felt like lace panties that if Al wasn't in a public place, she'd get down on her knees to examine more closely with her tongue. "How does that sound?"

Her grin stretched wide. "Like a party I wouldn't want to miss."

Chapter Twenty-One

CC parked her car in the driveway behind Al's rental and took a moment to reflect over the past month, over the ups and downs that had brought her to the edge of this cliff, about to take a leap she couldn't have imagined at the start of the holiday season. She couldn't have guessed that the salt-and-pepper spitfire who had approached her table at SFO would be her companion on the roller coaster of the past month, would be the person holding her hand as she jumped tonight.

Her belly somersaulted with excitement, the earlier worry that had nagged her all month gone. Her clients were happy, and CC was pretty damn sure Al was going to make her a happy woman tonight too. Hopefully for many more nights to come. Was there a risk the fire between them might burn out? Sure, she had to be realistic, but for the first time in six years she wanted to walk through that fire. She didn't want to hide from herself, from her needs, or from the woman whose needs she hoped to help meet too. They'd only known each other a month and had a lot more to learn, but what CC knew of Al already included the open arms and giant heart she wrapped around her loved ones, and it made CC want to be counted among them. Made her want to help Al feel at home here in New Orleans too.

She snagged the gift box off the passenger seat and pushed her car door open. Following the instructions from Al's text that afternoon, she bypassed the walkway to the front of the house and instead approached the back gate. She punched in the code, swung it open, and followed the stone path around the garage, toward what she recalled was the pool and back of the house. She'd barely cleared the garage corner when a whistle drew her attention back toward Al's office.

CC nearly dropped the box in her hands. The space formerly known as Al's office had been completely transformed. Electric candles of varying shapes and sizes flickered from every surface, vases of fresh flowers dotted the bookshelves and wet bar, and the office chair and desk had been removed, the chaise now positioned front and center.

And in the middle of it sat Al, her legs crossed and arms stretched across the back cushions. She wore a black silk robe cinched at the waist. The fabric parted over her crossed knees to reveal leather garters and sheer stockings; it gapped at the top to reveal nothing but pale skin. CC recalled Al's words from their flight all those weeks ago—the mental image she'd painted of her breasts spilling out of a leather corset—and CC hoped like hell that was what was hiding under the silk.

"Eyes up here, Red."

She whipped her gaze to the dark one that glowed in the candlelight. "You wore that knowing exactly where my eyes would go."

Al's answering smirk was devastating. CC whimpered, and if not for the box in her hands, she would have either clenched her own breasts or reached between her legs to relieve the pressure there.

"I'll take care of that soon," Al said, as if reading her mind. "I promise. But we have a few things to go over first."

"Like?"

Her eyes dipped to the gift box. "Like what you've brought me."

CC closed her eyes and inhaled deep, grasping for composure. Praying for the strength to approach the living, breathing temptation on the chaise in front of her and not immediately drop to her knees. When she thought herself steady enough, she opened her eyes again and approached. "Since you're staying in town, I wanted to be sure you had what you needed for life in New Orleans."

Al's expression softened, her eyes crinkling at the corners and her smirk smoothing into a fond smile. "You didn't have to get me anything."

"I wanted to." She handed the box over, then lowered herself onto the chaise beside Al, a leg folded under her.

Al's dark eyes shot to the gap in her skirt, then to the part of her thighs the position created.

"What'd I do?" CC feigned innocence.

"Trouble," Al muttered as she dragged her gaze away and back to the box on her lap. She removed the bow, lifted the lid, then drew out the first of four items wrapped in tissue paper.

And laughed out loud at the plastic cup of beads.

"For Mardi Gras season," CC said.

The laughter continued as she unwrapped a flashlight —"For hurricane season," CC explained—then a black and gold neck fan—"For football season and the everything-but-three-months-of-the-year season."

She pulled out the last item, her brows furrowing as she no doubt noticed the much lighter weight than the others. But it was the gift that got the loudest laugh of all. "For the needling Greg season," CC explained as Al wove the green and white Tulane-branded neck scarf through her fingers. "And because you and your ties have been torturing me from day fucking one."

"It's perfect." Grin turning wicked, Al looped it around her neck, quickly tied it, then moved to tuck the ends inside her robe.

CC batted her hands away and instead used the ends to draw Al closer. "I need to kiss you."

"Then kiss me."

CC didn't hesitate, bringing her mouth down on Al's and thrusting her tongue between Al's lips, tangling and tasting, wanting what she'd resisted for far too long. Wanting more. She levered up on the leg beneath her and threw the other over Al's lap, straddling her as she wrapped both arms around her neck, kissing her fill. Al's hands coasted up her thighs, under the skirt, and over her hips, squeezing her ass cheeks. CC rocked her hips and gasped, the drag of Al's garters and nylons on the backs of her thighs, the dig of her nails into her cheeks the best kind of torture. "I need you," she pleaded against Al's lips.

"I need to give you something first."

CC drew back, expecting Al's wicked grin, and was surprised to find her expression serious. Maybe even a touch hesitant. "What is it?" CC asked as she settled back on Al's thighs.

Al plucked a single sheet of paper out from behind one of the chaise cushions. She held the paper out to CC. "I want you to read this before we go any further in case it changes how we proceed."

With that lead-in, the only reason CC's hand didn't shake when she took the paper from Al was because she recognized the letterhead from other documents the past week.

Rosin Hospitality.

She read through the letter, eyes widening with each line, her brain struggling to wrap itself around what it meant, her insides an equal mess of excitement and . . . fear, maybe? She reached Tyler's signature at the bottom, then glanced back up at Al, who was tucking the scarf into her robe pocket. "You're offering me a job?"

"Rosin Hospitality is." She tapped the logo at the top of the page. "And I had nothing to do with this. It was all Sloan and Tyler. They were impressed at how efficiently you handled the deal last week. And with operations expanding, they're ready to bring legal in-house. They asked me to be general counsel, and I said no. I want to start winding down. But you . . ." She covered one of CC's hands. "You're exactly what a growing hospitality company needs."

CC read over the letter again. The offer was for more than MRM currently paid her, was more than her share as an equity partner would be if MRM ever made her one. The position location was flexible, and it included the ability to bring an associate general counsel on board. Maybe Brynn would want to join her? But she'd be asking Brynn to come off partnership track early, and she would have to leave her own book of business behind. "I need time to think about this," she told Al. "It wasn't anywhere on my radar."

"But I can tell Ty you'll consider it?"

She nodded. "I can't not. It's right in my wheelhouse, it's a very queer-friendly company, and I could bring Brynn. I just . . . never seriously considered in-house before."

"Law schools don't like to tell us about the nonfirm options." She lowered her voice in a conspiratorial whisper. "Doesn't pad their bottom line as well." CC chuckled, and Al slipped the paper out of her hands. "Take all the time you need, but I wanted you to know about the offer before we went any further tonight. RH is my family's company, but I'll have zero say over your job or how you do it. Tyler would be your boss." She clasped both of CC's hands in hers. "That said, you and I are about to enter into a Domme/sub relationship, and if this job changes those power dynamics too much for you, then we stop right now. Mind you, I have no intention of letting it. I will never hold one or the other over you, I promise, but you have to trust that promise, CC—*completely*—or this"—she gestured between them—"doesn't work."

CC closed her eyes again, inhaling deep as she gathered her thoughts and words. She only needed a moment, the differences so stark between Quinn and Al, between the past and the present. She opened her eyes and clenched Al's hands in hers. "Thank you for recognizing that and for offering me the out. Which only proves how good a Domme you will be."

"But if I'm ever not—"

"I will tell you. That's my promise in return." She withdrew her hands and leaned forward, hands braced on the back of the chaise, as she trailed a line of kisses along Al's neck. "Now can we get to those other promises you made me?"

Al smiled against her lips. "Which ones were those?"

She nipped Al's ear. "The ones where you make me scream."

Chapter Twenty-Two

"Scream, huh?" Al said. "In that case, I have three options for you."

CC left her hands braced on either side of Al but drew back enough to meet her hooded gaze. "I don't need options, Al. I need your fingers in my cunt, like, yesterday." Al lightly popped her ass cheek, and CC hissed. "Not helping."

"You won't come until I tell you to." Al waited for her nod before continuing. "Option one, I close the office doors, activate the blackout glass, and fuck you on this couch."

And that was only option one? *Fuck.*

CC squirmed, desperate to relieve the ache between her legs, the gusset of her leotard stretching tight over her center. Al slid a hand down, cupping her, pressing up with the heel of her palm where CC needed it most. CC didn't dare rut against it, though, not wanting the touch to go away. "Option two?"

"I send a text to the group of people enjoying drinks on my front patio and let them know the show is on."

A thrill raced down CC's spine. "The show?"

"Folks like us, who like to watch and be watched, and they will be watching from the living room windows as I fuck you out here."

CC wouldn't have been able to stop the roll of her hips if her life depended on it. Thank fuck Al seemed equally turned on, the heel of her palm skating enticingly over CC's clit. "I'll show them how lucky I am to have such an amazing, powerful woman as my sub."

CC was ninety-nine percent sure she was going with option two, but she needed to hear it all. "Option three?"

"I tell them to go away, or let them listen, as I take you upstairs to my bedroom and you ride my strap-on like I promised the other night."

"Fuck." CC pushed off the back of the couch, upright in Al's arms, her head thrown back as she continued to rock her hips, rutting her clit against the pressure Al applied. She palmed her breasts, kneading them like in the fantasy Al had previously painted, and Al's groan matched her own.

"Yeah, baby," Al whispered against the underside of her chin. "You like the sound of that." She popped two of the snaps on the gusset—the sound, the sensation sent a shock straight to CC's clit, a second shock on its heels as Al dipped two fingers into CC's soaked center. "Oh, feel how wet you are. All for me."

"Yes."

She glided slick fingers along either side of her clit. "Tell me which you want, CC."

"Option two."

"Figured you might." She kissed along CC's throat. "There's a New Year's Eve party tomorrow night at another house. They can hear me fuck you then." Al's two fingers dove back inside her, and CC's muscles contracted around them. "Greedy," Al murmured.

"For you." CC righted her head, pleased to see Al's face as flushed as hers felt. "And deal."

Al withdrew her fingers, and CC whimpered. "Patience," Al said with a chuckle. She dug her phone out from behind a cushion but paused before sending the **We're a go** text she'd typed. "Safe words?" she asked CC. "Mine are green, yellow, red. Yours?"

"Whiskey for green, tequila for yellow, vodka for red."

Al rolled her eyes and hit send on the text. "Explains so much. Limits?"

"No degradation or humiliation."

"Is calling me ma'am that to you? You've used it before, but I need to be sure."

CC shook her head. "No, ma'am."

Al smirked. "Quit trying to distract me. What about pain?" CC opened her mouth to respond, but Al added first, "Be honest. Remember, I'm not a sadist, but I do need to know how hard I can squeeze these." She palmed the side of CC's left breast, and CC's eyes fluttered closed again as she relished the touch.

"Seven out of ten," CC answered.

"And the spank earlier was okay?"

"Yes, ma'am." She groaned as Al spread her whole hand over her breast and swiped her thumb across the top curve. "Please."

"Last question, I promise." It better have been because as her hand glided south, down between CC's legs to open the rest of the snaps, CC was already careening toward the edge. "When's the last time you were tested? Because I plan to feast down here tonight."

"Last month, negative. No one since."

"Last spring for me, negative, no partners since."

CC whipped up her gaze, disbelieving.

"Don't look so surprised. We both work like madwomen." She tilted forward, stealing a deep, plundering kiss, her hand tangling in CC's hair and giving a tug that made every part of CC feel like it was bursting at the seams. "No work tonight," Al said, drawing back, then with a pat to CC's thigh, ordered, "Stand."

CC unfolded herself from Al's lap and stepped back, glancing over her shoulder at the house. Where before it had been dark, the kitchen and living area were now cast in low light, and several people milled about with wine glasses in hand. No one was watching them yet, but CC could feel the wave of sexual energy from here. It sped up her pulse and raised the hairs on her arms, adrenaline—the good kind—pumping.

"Your drink of choice?" Al asked.

At the prompt for consent, CC returned her attention to her Domme. "Whiskey, ma'am."

"Good." On her feet now too, Al stepped around her,

then jutted her chin toward the chaise. "Climb onto the couch. Sit on the corner, at the top, facing the house."

CC moved to take off her shoes, but Al clicked her tongue against her teeth. "Nope, leave those beauties on. I'll help you get into position." She held her steady while CC navigated her way onto the solid couch corner. She wedged one heel between a cushion and the couch arm and braced the other on the middle seat cushion. Spread for all the world to see, only the flimsy end of the gusset, the organza shirt, and Al blocking her from view.

"Drink of choice?" Al asked again.

"Whiskey," CC answered without hesitation.

Smiling, Al carefully tucked the gusset up under the front of the leotard and draped the organza back behind her knees, baring her completely. "Keep your hands on the couch," she said before stepping back. Still in front of her, she turned toward the house. Over her shoulder, CC watched their audience come to attention, all of them held rapt as Al untied and dropped her robe, black silk fluttering to the floor.

CC's mouth went dry, her gaze traveling from Al's heels, up the seams of her stockings, along the leather garters that bisected the back of her thighs and bare ass cheeks, a tiny thong nestled in her crack, then along the zipper of her leather corset that ran from the small of her back to her shoulder blades. Low enough that—when Al turned—CC could see that her breasts were spilling out of the top of the corset, just like she promised.

CC groaned and spread her legs more, hips thrusting

forward. Fuck, she needed to rub her clit to relieve the pressure that was about to blow.

"Keep your hands on the couch," Al ordered, sensing her distress. "I'll take care of you, I promise." She kicked off her heels, stepped onto the chaise, and palmed the underside of her right breast. "I'm going to feed this to you and tell you how to treat it. Make no other movements." She held the tit against CC's parted lips, and CC breathed hot air over it, smiling as Al shivered. "Slow licks around the nipple. Takes a little more work for it to stiffen." CC pressed her lips more firmly against the darker pink of Al's areola, then swirled her tongue, above, under, and along each side of her nipple, like Al had teased her clit earlier.

"Yeah, that's it." The low timbre of Al's voice, the slight shake to it, filled CC with joy, with satisfaction that she was returning the care Al was showing her. Stoking Al's desire as much as Al was stoking hers. "Suck now, gently, and flick the nipple with your tongue." CC increased the pressure with her lips, applying suction as she flicked the tip of her tongue over the numb. Al's hand tangled in her hair, holding her there, humming in content. A vibration CC felt all the way to her core. She repeated the teasing lick and suck again.

"No playing favorites," Al said as she leaned back and switched her hold, feeding her other tit to CC. "Gentle licks and flicks. I want this one as good and stiff as the first." Her hand fisted in CC's hair again, and CC lost herself in the pleasure she was giving, in the way the soft skin around Al's nipple wrinkled, the way her nipple stiffened as CC continued to tease and torture it. She was so caught up in sensation that she gasped when another entered the picture, Al's other hand between her legs again. CC slammed her tongue up, catching Al's nipple against the roof of her mouth before it slipped from her lips.

Al chuckled. "You're good with that tongue." She spread CC open, swiped her fingers through the moisture there, then glided her fingers around her clit again, mimicking CC's motions. "Oh, baby, you're soaked. Is this for me?"

"Yes, ma'am," she mumbled around Al's breast.

"I want to stand back and see. Will you show me?"

She carefully released Al's tit. "Yes, ma'am."

CC clutched the back of the couch, having to balance again without Al's counterweight to lean on. Standing, Al's gaze swept over CC like a brand, burning hottest where it landed on her center. "Look at you, gorgeous and glistening wet for me. Your cunt's so hungry."

"So fucking hungry."

"So powerful." She lifted her heated gaze, catching Al's. "Will you show them too?"

Them.

Their audience.

CC had forgotten all about them, so caught up in Al. At the reminder, she grew hotter, her clit throbbed harder. She nodded.

"Spread your legs as wide as you can," Al said.

CC pushed her right leg out, all the way to the chaise arm, and, with her left heel, kicked over the middle back cushion and planted her foot in it. Al smiled wide, full of pride that filled CC with the same. "Drink?"

"Whiskey."

"You're fucking stunning, CC."

Al stepped out of the way, and CC got her first clear look at the house. Of the gazes locked on her, of the people tangled together against the window and on the couches and chairs turned toward the windows. Between glances, they were kissing and touching, turned on by her and Al.

"Everyone in that room wishes they were me," Al said as she circled behind CC, her hot breath coasting over the crook of CC's neck. She wove an arm under CC's, over her thigh, and between her legs, holding her there. "They wish all this was for them. And some of it is, isn't it?" Al had to have felt the blast of heat, the ripple of excitement her words caused. "Show 'em your tits too. Take them out of that dress like I told you to the other night." She stepped closer, front against CC's back, bracing her. "I've got you."

CC released the couch, blood rushing back into her hands. She stretched her fingers, once, twice, then lifted them to the neckline of her dress so she could drag it down with the cups of her bra, creating a shelf below her bared breasts.

"Play with them," Al said. "Show them how you like to be teased while I tease you too."

CC kneaded and rolled her tits, and behind her, Al dipped and flicked her fingers between CC's legs and moved in a slow wave. She rocked their bodies together, taking her along for the ride. With her words too, she painted erotic works of art, narrating the scene they were creating and witnessing. "You see that woman in the chair in the lace one-piece?" CC found her through the haze of lust, a woman with tan skin, long dark hair, and in a purple lace lingerie that opened in a V down the center, from her shoulders to below her belly button. She was seated in one of the oversize chairs, her breasts spilling out of the lace, her legs thrown over the arms, spread like CC. "I bet her cunt is as wet as yours. You see how dark the lace of her crotch is? Watch the movement of her hand, CC. She's stuffing herself full, wishing her fingers were the ones inside you." Al shoved three fingers inside her, and CC grunted, her hips shooting off the couch, riding Al's hand. "I bet she wishes she could taste you as much as I want to."

CC's eyes fluttered closed, and she dropped her head back onto Al's shoulder. "Mouth, please."

She kissed a path down her neck, then flicked her tongue in the sensitive spot behind CC's ear, making her tremble. "You want mine on you?"

"Please."

"Lower yourself onto the cushions."

CC levered herself off the corner and down onto the chaise proper. She scooted back into the corner, one leg hanging off the front, the other propped on the cushions. Al circled in front of her, and CC had a moment of how-the-fuck-did-I-get-this-lucky. The woman in front of her was gorgeous, her body poured into leather and nylon, her nipples hard and skin flushed, her eyes full of dark, delicious thoughts. CC shook her head in wondrous disbelief. "You are so fucking hot."

"Says the firecracker laid out like a snack." Al put a

knee to the couch and braced a hand in the cushion behind CC. With the other, she palmed CC's breast. "I bet everyone in the house up there wishes they could fill their hands full of these tits. Suck on them too." She dipped her head, lifted with her hand, and closed her mouth around CC's nipple, sucking hard.

"Fuck yes." CC drove her hands into Al's gray curls and held on tight, loving the stimulation, the intimacy, the way Al stopped just shy of CC's pain threshold. "More, please."

She moved to the other breast and repeated the delicious torture. "I could feast here all night."

"Appetizers," CC panted. "Don't fill up." She flicked a glance down to where she wanted Al to carry through with her promise to feast.

"Oh, you thought this was appetizers? No, baby, that was the amuse-bouche." She regretfully drew back and straightened onto her knee. "Put a hand on your cunt, but do not touch your clit." CC did as told, hissing at the nearby bundle of nerves that was ready to explode. "Trust me," Al said. "It'll be worth it. Get those fingers good and wet for me."

While she did that, Al stood the rest of the way up and turned toward the house. She spread her legs shoulder width apart, tilted slightly forward, then reached behind her and spread her ass cheeks. "Now smear yourself on my hole."

"Penetration?"

"No, just teasing. I want those people watching to see how powerful you are. See you bring me to the edge too."

It was a genius move, a good Domme giving her sub time to come back down from the edge. Except it only worked for so long, Al's "fuck" and "baby," her "so good" and "more, please" working CC back up.

CC had to wave the white flag. Or rather, yellow. "Tequila."

Al straightened at once and turned to face her, blocking the voyeurs inside the house from seeing. "What do you need?"

"I'm at my limit. I want to follow your orders, but I can't keep staring at my fingers on your hole while you curse and mutter my name and not come."

Al chuckled, then put a knee to the chaise again and braced both arms on either side of CC. She leaned in for a slow, soft kiss, affection and care flowing between them. "Thank you for telling me." She drew back, smiling. "Hold the back of the couch until you're ready to let go." The gentle kisses continued south, over CC's chest, adorning her breasts, down her stomach and over the material of her dress, and—as Al went to her knees on the floor in front of the chaise—inside both of CC's thighs. Until finally, Al placed a soft kiss on CC's aching center. The gentleness only lasted a second, though, before she shoved her tongue inside and feasted, exactly as promised. CC tipped back her head, moaning as she rode the pleasure Al gave her with her tongue and fingers, bringing her swiftly to the edge. Standing at the cliff, she righted her gaze and opened her eyes. Seeing all the gazes locked on them, CC felt power surge through her. She tangled a hand in Al's hair, and Al's closed over hers; CC jumped, her climax exploding in a scream she was sure the folks in the house—and the neighbors—heard.

When she landed on solid ground once more, Al was grinning up at her, lips glistening, eyes shining with pride. "You are amazing, Carrington."

CC hauled her up into a kiss, sharing all the joy she felt, all the gratitude to Al for helping her take back what she'd missed so much the past six years. A part of herself that she had lost and found again with this incredible woman. "You are too. Now, can I make you come?"

"Someone wants dessert?"

"Fuck yes."

Laughing, Al stood, propped a foot on the cushion by CC's leg, and pulled aside the front of the thong between her legs. "Dessert is served."

CC didn't need to be told twice. She lunged forward, mouth seeking out Al's cunt, getting the taste she'd been craving for weeks. It was everything she'd dreamed of. Everything incredible about the woman who had challenged her, who had worked with her to find solutions, who had drawn CC out of her shell and back to herself. She licked and sucked her fill, added fingers when she could sense Al racing toward her end. When she tipped into CC, one hand in her hair, the other going to the back of the couch, CC made a final play, flicking the strap of the thong over her clit like Al had promised her on the plane weeks ago.

"Fucking naughty," Al cursed on a gasp, then tensed, her climax colliding against CC's lips and around her fingers.

After, CC helped her down to the chaise with her, their legs and arms a tangle. Al hummed and nuzzled her breasts. "I can't wait for the party tomorrow night. You're going to be fucking amazing."

CC's gaze drifted again toward the house, and she smiled at the pleasure on display there. She'd caused that, and she hadn't done it alone; she propped an elbow on a pillow and gazed fondly down at the woman who'd done it with her. "I can't wait for all the nights with you."

Reviews are an invaluable tool when it comes to spreading the word about great reads. Please consider leaving an honest review for *Over a Barrel* on your favorite review site.

Thank you for reading!

Acknowledgments

Holiday cheer for all, especially for Al and CC! I've been waiting to tell this story for what feels like forever. From the initial nugget of an idea years ago, to the cover photo I likewise bought years ago, to the mentions of Al in other stories building up to this one. I'm so happy her and CC's story is finally out in the world for all to enjoy. And also yay for more of this fun found family. Team Plaid FTW!

Many thanks to Cate Ashwood for the cover and to Wander Aguiar for the stunning cover photo of Emily. Thanks as well to Kim and Laura for the beta reads, to Adam for reining in my unwieldy modifiers, and to Lori for her always excellent proofing.

Last but not least, thank you readers for embracing this foodie family and all my foodie love. It's been lovely to start and finish this year with such tasty meals!

Best Play

About the Author

Layla Reyne is the author of *What We May Be* and the *Agents Irish and Whiskey, Changing Lanes,* and *Table for Two* series. She writes sexy, intense LGBTQIA+ romance featuring competent adults in kitchens, sports arenas, car chases, and other high-stakes situations. Whether it's adrenaline-fueled suspense, rival athletes, vampires and shifters in alt-realms, or love mixed with mouth-watering foodie goodness, queer folks finding happily-ever-afters is guaranteed.

You can find Layla at laylareyne.com, in her reader group on Facebook—Layla's Lushes, and at the following sites:

facebook.com/laylareyne

instagram.com/laylareyne

bookbub.com/authors/layla-reyne

tiktok.com/@laylareyne

www.ingramcontent.com/pod-product-compliance
Lightning Source LLC
Chambersburg PA
CBHW072135300726
48975CB00003B/1075

* 9 7 9 8 9 8 6 9 2 2 9 9 7 *